Nanny Confidential

For my Gran

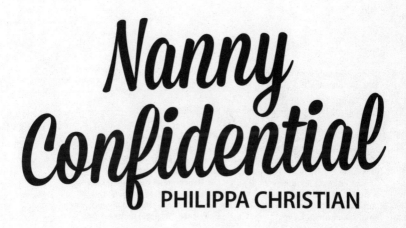

Nanny Confidential

PHILIPPA CHRISTIAN

ALLEN&UNWIN

SYDNEY · MELBOURNE · AUCKLAND · LONDON

This edition published in 2016
First published in 2015

Allen & Unwin
83 Alexander Street
Crows Nest NSW 2065
Australia
Phone: (61 2) 8425 0100
Email: info@allenandunwin.com
Web: www.allenandunwin.com

Cataloguing-in-Publication details are available
from the National Library of Australia
www.trove.nla.gov.au

ISBN 978 1 76029 119 8

Printed in Australia by McPherson's Printing Group

10 9 8 7 6 5 4 3 2 1

1

As I sprinted down Rodeo Drive, racing to get to a beautician's appointment, with a child bouncing in a Bugaboo pushchair and a Louis Vuitton handbag slung over my shoulder, I kept a watchful eye out for paparazzi. Those guys are never far behind me. Neither is my personal bodyguard, who I could hear huffing, puffing and muttering, 'Why couldn't she just bring the damn chauffeur like a normal person?'

The problem is, having a chauffeur-driven Mercedes at your beck and call isn't considered 'normal' where I come from. I might look like the stereotypical Hollywood yummy mummy, with my blonde hair swishing in the breeze and my diamond watch glittering in the sunlight, but appearances can be deceptive.

In fact, the child isn't mine, the handbag was a freebie and it's the three-year-old girl in the stroller who is booked in for a facial and a pedicure. I'm just there to act as her chaperone.

My name is Lindsay Starwood and I'm an elite VIP nanny. Although nobody knows my name, they certainly know the names of my employers. I've cared for the children of the richest parents on the planet, from presidents to movie stars, oil barons, hotel heirs and supermodels. I've worked for so many celebrities that gossip magazines are like my version of Facebook—that's the way I keep up to date with the lives of my past and present celebrity bosses. My CV reads like the Hollywood Walk of Fame.

In a sense I am rich and famous by proxy, because being linked to a famous family opens every door in the city. I can get a table at any restaurant, as long as I'm with the children. I've flown on private jets and lived in a mansion the size of two football pitches. And that's really only the tip of the iceberg.

I've seen wealth that I could never have dreamed of back when I was growing up in a small country town in Australia, but my job isn't quite the Mary Poppins fantasy that you'd imagine. It's a labour of love and a test of endurance. These parents' expectations are high, and thankyous are hard to come by. I'm often asked if the children I care for are spoilt, but they're really just following the examples set by their elders. Let's just say I've never come across a baby who was born a diva—it's a case of nurture over nature. I once knew a mother who named her daughter 'Your Highness'. How was she supposed to grow up to be well-adjusted with that on her birth certificate?

As a VIP nanny you see and hear it all, from domestic arguments to dodgy business deals, unwanted pregnancies and the aftermath of plastic surgery. Oh, but the handcuffs are golden! I'm only twenty-seven years old and earn up to $500,000 a year, without paying any living expenses. I live in the lap of luxury, holiday at the best hotels in the world and have a wardrobe that's worth a large fortune. On top of my generous pay packet, I have been 'tipped' with expensive jewellery, vouchers for plastic surgeries, a convertible BMW and even a prize-winning pony that I could keep in the family's stables.

So how did a small-town girl from rural Australia find herself caring for the tots of Tinseltown? I'm not a wannabe actress who came to Hollywood chasing stardom and then had to find a backup plan when it all fell through, if that's what you're thinking. It sounds like a cliché but I just genuinely love children, and they seem to love me too.

Take the three-year-old currently bouncing around in my stroller. Lavender Appleby is one of the six daughters of movie director Cameron Appleby and his soap star wife, Alysha. Sorry, that's '*Sir* Cameron Appleby *the third*' to you and me.

I've only been working for the Appleby family for a fortnight since leaving my previous role and yet, last night as I tucked Koko in to bed, she wrapped her arms around my neck and whispered, 'Lindsay, will you be my mommy, and mommy can be my nanny?'

Either she'd already grown attached to me in the past two weeks—it does happen—or the mature little girl had done the maths and realised that if her mum were her nanny, rather than a celebrity and socialite, then she'd be more likely to spend quality time with her children. That morning on my way out the door Alysha had given me one instruction: 'Don't let the children nap during the day, nanny. When I get home from work I need them to be too tired to ask me to play with them.' Truly unbelievable but, depressingly, not unusual.

That's why doing my job, and doing it well, is so important. A nanny is one of the few constants in the lives of richie-rich children, and it's rewarding to see the difference I can make to their wellbeing.

I've always been drawn to babies, ever since I was given a bag of flour with stick-on eyes as part of a school project and was charged with the task of keeping it 'alive' for a week. I was so frustrated by the other students' apathetic attitudes towards their bags of flour that I ended up setting up a corner of the classroom as my 'nursery' for looking after everyone else's 'babies'. Unfortunately, as an only child, the number of real babies in my vicinity was limited. I was born in a country town called Hamilton in south-east Australia, which only has a population of just over 8000 people. We knew absolutely everyone in our town, and there were only three girls in my year at school.

That's why, when I was fourteen years old, my parents decided to move to Melbourne to give me a better education. When I was growing up they ran the local convenience store, which sold everything from groceries to camping equipment. It also had a coffee shop in the back, and they were the first to offer computers with internet back in the days when computers were still mystical. They might have been from a small town, but they were always thinking ahead, and they weren't shy of hard work. I remember my dad getting up at the crack of dawn to help our neighbours milk their cows before working an eight-hour shift at the cafe. I also remember thinking it was unfair that, for all the hours he was working, we couldn't afford to turn the hot water on more than one day a week.

I had a very sheltered childhood, in a sense. I wasn't allowed to watch television for more than one hour a night, and I didn't set foot in a cinema until we moved to Melbourne. On the first weekend after we relocated to the city, my mum took me to see *The Princess Diaries*. My dad decided to stay at home after checking the price of the tickets. I wasn't allowed popcorn, but we brought Vegemite sandwiches from home. I was the only person in the audience who stood up and cheered at the end of the movie, because I found it so spellbinding. This was probably because my childhood entertainment up to that point had revolved around picking blackberries and skimming stones in the river.

How times have changed since then. I've been on countless movie sets, watched music videos being filmed and sat in green rooms next to my childhood idols. The novelty soon wears off when you're trying to keep a group of kids amused without getting under the feet of producers, directors and actors.

When I was younger my ignorance of popular culture probably worked in my favour. When I got a babysitting job, aged just twelve, I was vaguely aware that the parents I worked for were 'somebodies', but I wasn't as starstruck as my school friends would have been. My mother worked as a shop assistant in a clothing store and met Eliza Shawshank when she came in to buy a hat for the Melbourne horse races. They'd got talking in the changing room and Mum had mentioned that she had a teenage daughter. The following Friday I was dispatched to a mansion on the other side of the city, left in charge of three children, and told I could help myself to anything in the fridge. I had my first taste of caviar that night, and spat it straight into the garbage.

I was naturally nosey and toured the house when the children were sleeping, piecing together clues about the family's background. The first giveaway was the recording studio in the basement, where the walls were decorated with gold and silver records. Above the children's beds was a framed photograph of them with Michael Jackson. In another photo they were hugging Kylie Minogue. On the mantelpiece in the living room was a pile of sparkling invitations to parties taking place across the world, including the Grammys and the MTV Europe Awards.

Eliza and Jason Shawshank certainly had an active social life and, for almost two years, I spent every Friday and Saturday night at their house. I developed a bit of a girl-crush on Eliza, to be honest. I used to arrive half an hour early so that I could sit on her bed and watch her get ready. It amazed me that a woman came around to do her hair and make-up. She always lets her six-year-old daughter choose her earrings to go with her outfit.

I went to a strict Catholic school, which didn't let students miss classes unless they presented a medical certificate. One day, I pulled a sickie so I could accompany the Shawshanks on a daytrip to Disney World in Florida over the weekend. Unfortunately I didn't realise that photographers followed them everywhere. That evening my teacher spotted me on the evening news boarding a private jet in Orlando, wearing a pair of Minnie Mouse ears. She wasn't impressed when I came in on Monday, with a note from my mother that claimed I'd had a stomach bug.

I had been planning to go to university to study child psychology, but as my final school exams rolled around, Eliza made me an offer. Would I be interested in moving in with the family and taking care of their children full time, as their nanny?

She then named a salary that, to an eighteen-year-old student, sounded like a fortune. A lot of my school friends were taking a gap year to travel around Europe. If I moved into the Shawshanks' mansion it would be like a working holiday. I'd heard my parents arguing about how they were going to be able to afford to send me to university and I didn't want my dad to have to get a second job.

'I'll just do it for a year,' I told my mum. 'I can save enough money to get myself through university without needing to get into debt.' Of course, it didn't work out like that. A year became a career and my university place was deferred and then given away.

Shortly after my nineteenth birthday an email arrived from the manager of a Hollywood actor who was planning a trip to Australia. He needed a nanny to take care of his four sons during their holiday and wondered if I'd fly to Sydney to stay with them on a yacht on the harbour.

I wasn't really looking for extra work but I wondered if the universe was sending me a message. When they asked for my fee I quadrupled my rate, just to see what they'd say. I told them my standard fee was $500, per child, per day, which meant I'd be paid $14,000 for a week's work.

I fully expected them to look elsewhere, and couldn't believe it when the agent emailed back. 'My client is happy with that fee,' it read. 'They will also cover your living expenses, including accommodation, travel and food, and provide you with an appropriate wardrobe.'

At the end of the holiday they asked me to return with them to Los Angeles and work for them. They already had a nanny, who later sued for unfair dismissal, as she only found out she'd been replaced when I walked into her bedroom carrying my suitcase. The Hollywood hiring process can be fast and fickle. I sometimes feel like I'm only just hanging on by my fingertips. But what other career would give you the perks of fame, without needing to actually be famous? I may work like a slave but I live like a queen.

•

'Lindsay, why is there a photo of Daddy without his clothes on, and what does "sexting" mean?'

This was the moment I knew I had to leave my last position and find another family to work for.

The hardest part of my job is watching kids grow up and realising they don't need me anymore. I give a little piece of my heart to every child, and when it's time for me to move on, that little boy or girl keeps it forever. Sadly, modern nannying is not the same as in Victorian times, when you were signed up at a baby's birth and still present at their wedding. My contracts are relatively short—anything from a week to eighteen months on average—because famous parents move around a lot. I work for musicians on tour and football stars on loan to different countries, and it's easier to recruit a new nanny every time they relocate. You can't take it personally; it's just part of the culture.

Sometimes it's my choice to leave a role, although this doesn't happen very often, as I pride myself on my loyalty. But every now and again working for a parent becomes so difficult that I have no choice but to plan an escape route. I hate it, because I feel as though I've let down the children, but sometimes it's necessary for the sake of my own sanity.

Before joining the Applebys, I had spent the previous three years working for the nineties boy-band heartthrob Steven Stavros and his far-too-forgiving wife, Barbie. Even if you're not a music fan, you're probably familiar with the sight of Steven's bare chest and Y-fronts. They've been splashed across the front pages of newspapers all over the world, thanks to his habit of sending indecent texts, and his inability to cover his tracks.

The first year of working for the Stavros family was

relatively quiet and peaceful. Then his band's fame began to wane, and his sex drive began to rocket.

'Isn't it terrible how the newspapers make up lies?' said my mum, every time I went home for Sunday lunch. 'As if he could hide these things from his wife. And how would he find the time to juggle all these women?'

I'd shrug and change the subject. Most people don't realise how much free time musicians have on their hands, especially when there's not an album to record or promote. They might have an occasional dance rehearsal or shopping-centre appearance, but spend a lot of time hanging around the house in between, buying boys' toys off the home shopping channel and browsing dating websites.

After a Las Vegas showgirl claimed they'd spent the night together during a bucks' party, the floodgates were opened for more girls to step forward. I knew that some of the stories were lies. Steven couldn't possibly have been in bed with those two strippers when he was playing Scattergories with the children and me that evening. However, he clearly wasn't squeaky clean, because one night he accidentally sent a text message to me that was meant for a girl called Lauren, inviting me back-stage after a gig. Steven didn't seem particularly embarrassed when he realised his case of mistaken identity.

Which of the stories were true and which were girls looking for a payout, probably only Steven and his genitals will ever know for certain. However, the kiss and tells came so frequently—and the details were so juicy—that for a while Steven was the prime target of every gossip columnist in the world.

One morning Steven called me into his study and handed me a mobile phone. I was puzzled.

'Umm, thanks, but I've already got an iPhone, Steven. You pay the bill, remember? Is this a new phone for one of the children?'

My boss shook his head. 'No, this is a second mobile phone for you to carry. It's pay-as-you-go, so it won't be traced by reporters. Only Barbie and I have the phone number, so if it rings it can only be us.'

The reason for the second phone soon became clear. It would only ring in one unique set of circumstances—when Steven had been caught in an illicit clinch (again!) and the children and I needed to prepare ourselves. Over time, I came to refer to the phone as the 'scandal hotline'.

I knew the drill when it rang. I even had overnight bags ready and waiting. I had to bundle the two children, aged three and seven, into my blacked-out Jeep and exit the house by the back gate, before the paparazzi arrived en masse. I then had to drive as fast as legally possible to the family's holiday home on the coast. They'd purchased the property under their cleaner's name to keep it a secret from the press.

I privately referred to this house, which was the seventh in their portfolio, as the 'infidelity bolthole'. When I was talking to the children I called it Hogwarts, which made sense, as it did have turrets and stone gargoyles around the swimming pool. The kids and I pretended that it was under an invisibility cloak, which was why they couldn't tell their friends that it existed. (You try explaining to a seven-year-old and a toddler that their father has been caught with his pants down, so they have to go into hiding.)

The length of our stay depended on the extent of the scandal and how easily Steven's publicity team could excuse it as idle gossip. A kiss-and-tell story could blow over in a week if they found a 'source' willing to discredit the stripper. If reporters had solid evidence, such as copies of 'sexts' or pornographic photographs, then the children and I could be camped out there for weeks, until the storm blew over. Their schoolteachers didn't question their absence. They used the gossip columns as a sick note, and knew exactly what was happening. They'd email me copies of the kid's assignments, politely not mentioning their dad's latest indiscretion.

During this time their parents came and went, often trailed by Steven's agent and manager, multiple personal assistants and a frazzled-looking publicist. I always knew that our solitary confinement would soon be over when I saw a photo of the couple in the newspaper putting on a 'united front' pose. This photograph would be staged by their publicity team and leaked to a magazine editor who Steven was friends with. It was usually a photo of the 'happy couple' arriving at a meeting hand-in-hand, or Steven giving Barbie a piggyback along a beach.

'Why do Mummy and Daddy never look that happy when they're with us?' asked three-year-old Zara one evening when her parents' faces popped up on the television. I paused as I tried to figure out how to explain the term 'fauxmance' to a toddler!

The shocking truth is that, after a decade working as a VIP nanny, I've started to think of incidents like this as normal. I've learnt that it's common for powerful men to have multiple wives—sometimes at the same time—and I've learnt that many women are prepared to ignore adultery in exchange for an opulent lifestyle.

This job makes you at best inquisitive and at worst totally distrusting of adults and their agendas. It can also leave you totally jaded when it comes to men and romance.

I've cared for the nine children of a Middle Eastern prince, juggling the orders of the father's three wives, who all lived together in the same palace. You wouldn't believe the conversations I've overheard women having with their girlfriends. 'He's freezing all the assets', 'How can I spend a million dollars in a day?' and 'Can you teach me how to knock a man out?' I've put children to bed with headphones on to drown out the sound of their parents screaming at each other. I've overheard a singer from a nineties boy band admit to his wife that the ballad everyone assumed was written about her was actually written about her best friend.

I worked for one famous father in Australia who told his wife he had to go to New York for business at short notice. She found out he was lying when she turned on the television and saw him on a dating show. He'd flown to America to film the episode. I overlooked all these misdemeanours and continued to work for the family, because it's even more important for a child to have the stabilising influence of a nanny when their parents are acting indecently.

I try not to judge, even though it's difficult sometimes. My priority is the children, and I see my role as being a steadying antidote to the surreal high of their parents' lives.

In spite of this, when Steven's youngest son, who was not even four years old, added the word 'sexting' to his vocabulary, I knew my time with the family was over. It was clear that Steven adored his kids despite his extracurricular activities. But it had become increasingly hard to protect, preserve and heal the children from the sins of their father.

When I received an email from the manager of Alysha Appleby asking if I'd be interested in attending an interview, the first thing I did was google the surname. I knew who both parents were—knowing the who's who of celebrities is part of my job description—but I wanted to know what I was getting into. 'Sir Cameron Appleby + affair' I typed in to Google. When it showed no relevant results I tried 'Sir Cameron Appleby + stripper'. Still nothing. This looked promising. When I searched for pictures of Sir Cam and Alysha at public appearances, strangely there seemed to be no photos of them together. However, there was also no hint of a dark and murky backstory. In hindsight I should have known better.

Over the years, I've learnt that the famous faces who are depicted as ogres by newspapers are usually the most kind-hearted in real life. I've also learnt that the angels, who seem to do no wrong, are sometimes just better at covering their tracks.

2

'Nanny! Where are you, *nanny*? How could you do this to *meeeee*?'

I was halfway through bathing two-year-old Koko when I heard the piercing scream coming from the kitchen. It was Monday morning, so this could only mean one thing. On the first day of the week the latest issues of the celebrity magazines hit the newsstands, and Alysha always spent the morning poring over each page of every magazine to see if she'd been mentioned.

Sadly, this task set the atmosphere for the entire week. If a magazine had included a flattering picture of Alysha in a bikini, usually Photoshopped to within an inch of its life and leaked by her agent, then my boss would be happy and the house would be peaceful. An unflattering photo resulted in an unhappy mummy and flying cutlery, especially if an art director had drawn a 'ring of shame' around her cellulite or if a fashion editor had described a recent outfit as a 'style blooper'.

There was only one thing worse than being publicly ridiculed, and that was not being mentioned at all. A storm cloud would then hang over the house for days, because Alysha's bad mood was contagious. It was hard not to be pulled down with her.

On 'Magazine Monday' it was usually Alysha's poor assistant who was first in the firing line if she hadn't got any publicity. She'd sacked five PAs in as many months for reasons that included 'being prettier than I am' and accidentally putting full-fat milk in her coffee.

However, this morning it was my name being hollered up the spiral staircase to the children's wing of the mansion. '*Lindsay*, how could you do this to me?' she screamed again. 'Are you trying to ruin my *life*?'

As I pulled Koko from the bath and wrapped her in a Versace towel, I mentally ran through a list of possible crimes I might have committed. Had one of the children been photographed drinking a fizzy drink, instead of the brand of coconut water that Alysha was sponsored by? My previous boss had lost a million-dollar endorsement deal after he was snapped smoking a cigarette when he was meant to be the face of a range of nicotine patches.

But my offence was far worse in Alysha's eyes. As I entered the kitchen, my boss was pacing around the table, wrapped in a pink kimono that clashed with her furious face. Most of the drama in the household seemed to happen in this kitchen. It was where scripts were read, contracts were signed and arguments played out, despite the fact the house had two studies, four living rooms and a huge library.

'Look at it, *look at it*!' Alysha screamed, throwing a balled-up page from a magazine at my head. 'I cannot believe you did this to me.' I'm used to being yelled at and am well aware that Alysha is prone to exaggeration, so I didn't immediately panic. Instead I picked up the paper cannonball from where it had landed beside my feet and smoothed it out onto the kitchen table.

At first glance I couldn't see the problem. In fact, I thought it was a very flattering photograph of Alysha, taken at a shopping mall the previous week. I thought she would be happy—her hair was freshly styled, her new Marc Jacobs handbag was in the frame and she was doing the half-smile that she'd copied from Victoria Beckham and practised in front of the mirror every evening.

I thought the photograph would tick all of Alysha's boxes, until I looked a little more closely. *Ohh no!* I would have sworn aloud, if I hadn't conditioned myself not to use 'bad words' in front of the children.

It seemed my boss wasn't the only person in the household to have made it into the gossip pages that week. I had unwittingly become a tabloid building block. In the background of the photograph, you could clearly see me a few steps behind Alysha, pushing a four-child buggy, with the baby strapped to my chest in a sling and the oldest sister, Harlow, trotting next to me, hanging on to my shirt tail.

Now I understood why Alysha was so enraged. I'd committed a cardinal sin.

When you're a VIP nanny there is one golden rule— never, ever get snapped by the paparazzi. If you are accidentally photographed beside your boss, just make sure you don't look like a nanny. It's our job to blend in to the background and look like a passerby or a friend—a friend generous enough to carry all the shopping bags, push the stroller and handle every tantrum and nappy change while not speaking unless she is spoken to.

The truth is, most famous mothers hate being photographed with their hired help, especially when it comes to childcare. I worked for an actress in California who insisted I walk five metres behind her at all times, even when I was pushing her newborn baby in a pram. It's all part of the superwoman illusion that famous mums like to create. Alysha had once described herself in a magazine article as 'anti-nanny', despite the fact that she'd never changed a single diaper.

When I first moved to Hollywood, having a large entourage was seen as a sign of success and status. However, now it's far cooler to pretend you're low-maintenance and juggle the demands of a career and parenthood alone.

This is why, as I read the caption under the photograph, my heart sank even deeper into my stomach. 'Soap star Alysha Appleby needs help handling her brood. Six children under the age of nine would be a match for any mom,' it read. The reporter had probably written those words without thinking, not realising that she was pulling the pin of a grenade.

It might sound like an overreaction, but Alysha's over-sized family was, unfortunately, a bit of a sore point. With six daughters born almost a year apart, the press often joked she had a girl band in the making. However, there was another reason Alysha had been pregnant for almost a decade. It was the worst-kept secret in Hollywood that Sir Cameron was desperate for a son, and was determined to keep procreating until he got one.

When I accepted the job with the Applebys, I had been intrigued to see the relationship dynamic between Alysha and her husband, who was twenty-nine years her senior. But so far I hadn't had the chance, because, in eight months, I hadn't once met Sir Cameron. I wondered how the couple had time to make so many babies, when his life seemed to be split between far-flung movie sets and their holiday home in San Tropez.

Although Sir Cameron was always absent, there were telltale clues about his desperate desire for a son. In the basement of the mansion, next to a one-hundred-seater private theatre, was a playroom that was filled with gender-specific boys' toys, such as cars, guns and a huge electric tank that was once used as a prop on the set of *M*A*S*H*. On my first day, I'd been warned that this playroom was off limits to the other children (translation: off limits to females). Only the cleaners ever entered the 'blue playroom', to dust it.

Another clue was the book in Sir Cameron's study titled *The Top Boys' Names of the New Millennium*. When I flicked through the pages, someone had highlighted 'Valentino' and 'Oscar'. They had also highlighted and then crossed out 'Harper'. Obviously the Beckhams had beaten them to it.

Unfortunately, Sir Cameron's desire for a son had not gone unnoticed by his oldest daughters, who seemed all too aware that their gender was a disappointment. On my third day on the job I caught six-year-old Cherry (yes, Cherry Appleby—a name more suited to a smoothie than a person!) throwing a hundred-dollar note into the water fountain in the back garden. When I asked what she was doing she told me it was her weekly pocket money, and that she was making a wish. 'I wished for a baby brother,' Cherry told me solemnly, 'So that Mommy can stop crying because she doesn't have any hair.' I was puzzled until I questioned the little girl further and realised that she meant 'an heir'. It was an easy mistake to make.

Clearly, the Appleby's family tree was a bit of a touchy subject. This is why Alysha was especially upset by my magazine cameo. 'You've made me look like an unfit mother!' she screamed. 'I hired you because you're meant to be the James Bond of nannying. You're supposed to be invisible! Instead, here you are flaunting yourself at the cameras. Don't let me regret hiring you, Lindsay!'

There was nothing I could do but let her vent her fury. I knew from experience that arguing back isn't wise. Would you sling mud at the man who pays your wages? People had been fired in the Appleby household for much less.

'I'm very, very sorry, Alysha,' I grovelled. 'It won't happen again, I promise. In the future I'll make sure that I look less . . . nannyish.' I wasn't sure how exactly I'd do this, but I suspected my next pay packet depended on it.

•

'You're like an undercover agent,' cooed my mum during my weekly phone call home, as I relayed the story of Alysha's recent tantrum. I blushed at the compliment, until I realised that she was kidding. It's not that much of a stretch. I wouldn't admit this to just anyone, but I do feel like a secret agent sometimes. I'm certainly not just an 'overpriced babysitter', as one former friend called me.

On a daily basis I wear so many different hats that it sometimes makes me feel dizzy. I'm a surrogate mother, a teacher, a therapist, a nutritionist, a cleaner and a body-guard. In the last ten years I've completed a degree in child psychology online, and five dangerous driving courses to learn how to escape paparazzi. I've studied first aid, martial arts, self-defence and had to learn how to fire a shotgun. I was once told by an American movie star father, 'The more paparazzi you can hit with your car, the higher your pay packet.'

The skills needed to be a VIP nanny are weird, varied and always evolving. Just as I'm getting used to the needs of one family, I move on to another, who have their own special set of requirements.

Last year I was hired to take care of the newborn baby of a reality television star and her rapper fiancé. On the first day in the job I was told I had to learn to speak Gaelic, because the mother's great-great-great grandmother had Irish blood. 'How cool would it be if Flossy's first words were Gaelic?' she gushed, although she didn't have time to learn the language herself. She was too busy crashing her car and tweeting about her clothing line. When the baby was asleep I'd watch the Gaelic news to try to learn the basics, and I listened to a crash course language CD every night before I went to sleep. In the end the baby's first word was 'mama'. I convinced them it was said in an Irish accent. This is why I get grumpy when people think my job is easy.

My mum knows me well enough to sense when I am sulking. 'I bet you're sticking out your bottom lip, aren't you?' she teased. 'Don't be silly, love. I know your job is very complicated. I just don't want you to get too caught up in that strange Hollywood world. As your mother it's my responsibility to keep your feet on the ground.'

I often feel like I live on a different planet to my parents, who moved back to Hamilton shortly after I moved in with the Stavros family. My dad said he needed to be closer to my ageing grandmother, but I think that was a convenient excuse. They never felt at home in the city and had only ever moved to Melbourne for the sake of my education. My dad describes any town with more than one bank in the high street as the 'big smoke'.

I regularly invite my parents to visit me in Los Angeles but they haven't yet taken me up on the offer, despite the fact they could have a free holiday. When you're a nanny working in a foreign country it's common for your employment contract to include family visits. I negotiated a good deal with the Applebys—I am allowed six overseas visitors a year and Sir Cameron will pay for their flights, plus a hotel for them to stay in. I try not to feel offended when my parents repeatedly turn down the offer to see me. My mum's entire opinion of Los Angeles is based on one episode she watched of *Keeping Up with the Kardashians*. 'I don't want to go to a place where fish nibble on my feet,' she says, even though I keep telling her a fish pedicure isn't a prerequisite.

'Mum, you don't need to worry about keeping my feet on the ground,' I reassured her. 'I'm still the same girl from Hamilton. I'm just playing a character.'

I've found that, to survive working for a boss from hell, it's best to hide layers of your true personality. I wouldn't admit it to my mother, but I didn't recognise myself sometimes.

There was a silence, and then my mum changed the subject. 'Have you been on any nice bike rides recently?' she asked. 'Your dad and I had a lovely pedal along the river the other day. I've got your waterproof jacket here if you want me to send it over.'

I didn't want to mention I hadn't been on a bike in six years and that Alysha would probably sack me if I came to work in an anorak, especially one that I bought when I was thirteen years old and has ladybirds printed all over it, with mittens on strings hanging from the arm-holes.

For my last birthday my mum sent a care package of 'treats' to Los Angeles, which included a nightdress, my 'favourite' cheesy crisps and an Enid Blyton book. The nightie was three sizes too big, and I haven't eaten a cheese Dorito since one of my kids vomited a packet onto me. I did read the book to the children, though, and they loved it.

I sometimes feel like, in my mum's mind, I'm frozen in time. It makes me sad that she knows nothing about my world and I know so little about hers.

Every time we talk I fall back on the same safe subjects: the weather, her vegetable garden and the council's plans to rip up a local field to build a golf course. Although I try to muster up some outrage, I don't think it's convincing. I hate that our conversations are often punctuated with awkward silences, such as the one that was hanging over us now.

After a pause, my mum filled the void. 'Well, I'm all out of news. You probably find my life very boring compared to yours,' she apologised. 'There's nothing very eventful happening here. Your life does seem very exciting, so I'm sure you're happy.'

But she didn't sound at all sure. Something in her tone of voice made me suspect that she wasn't convinced. Or maybe I was just being paranoid. After all, what did I possibly have to complain about?

3

'Will, is it weird for your boss to ask you to get a bikini wax?' I asked my best friend back in Hamilton, who had known me since I was three years old. I knew Will's answer even before he snorted with laughter. I was glad I hadn't asked 'Is it weird that my boss has seen my vajayjay?' It was now the truth, but he didn't need to know that.

I had rung Will from a phone booth because I was paranoid about my emails and phone calls being intercepted. I'd started using payphones after the British phone-tapping scandal—I wasn't going to risk details of my bikini line turning up in a newspaper.

I desperately needed to talk to someone about my day, and Will was my oldest friend and favourite confidant. Even though I am constantly relocating for my job—six months working for Indian royalty, eight months in a Bermuda tax haven—I use Will as an anchor to my history when I get caught up in Planet Showbiz.

Only my best friend knows the 'real' me rather than Lindsay the professional, capable caregiver. Will knows my tells and my weaknesses, like the fact I rub the end of my nose when I'm nervous, that I'm terrified of multi-storey car parks and that I believed in Santa until I was fifteen years old. These kinds of secrets bind two adults together forever.

That's why the first person I reached out to after losing the last shred of my dignity was Will. I had spent the morning in a torture chamber masquerading as a beauty parlour, being plucked, poked and preened into a Stepford Nanny.

It might sound like a treat but it was far from relaxing. What made it worse was that I felt like I'd been ambushed by Alysha. Yes, my bush had been ambushed! The first thing I knew about my waxing appointment was when I received an email confirming my 'intimate overhaul'.

From: holly@beautybynumbers.com
To: lindsay.starwood@gmail.com
Subject: Your Ultimate Grooming Package

Dear Ms Starwood,

Congratulations on taking the first step to a beautiful new you!

At the request of Mrs Alysha Appleby, we have scheduled your appointment for 6 a.m. on Wednesday 25 March.

The Ultimate Grooming Package takes approximately four hours to complete and includes a Brazilian wax, underarm lasering, teeth whitening, foot Botox, a coffee enema and a thirty minute session in our anti-ageing oxygen chamber.

Please do not eat for 90 minutes before your session, as this can result in nausea.

Yours flatteringly,
Holly Sheen
Chief Beautician

Not only had Alysha booked the appointment for the crack of dawn, so that it didn't interrupt my normal duties, but she also insisted on coming to the spa with me. I assumed she'd sit in the waiting room or have a treatment of her own, but when my name was called my boss followed me into the treatment room and positioned herself on a stall at the foot of the table.

'Umm, Alysha, you might not want to sit there,' I said, 'You do know that I'm having a bikini wax. From that angle, you'll be able to see . . . everything.'

She didn't look at all embarrassed. 'Of course I know that. That's why I'm here,' she huffed. 'It's always good to have a second opinion, and I have very high standards when it comes to personal grooming.'

I suspected I was being put to the test, and this was Alysha's payback for the paparazzi photograph. I had promised, after all, that I would try to look less like a nanny, so she was giving me a makeover. I just wish she hadn't come along to witness my transformation.

I inwardly cursed eight-year-old Harlow, who had walked in on me in the shower the week before and then announced over breakfast with her mother, 'Lindsay, why do you have hair where Mommy doesn't?' It wasn't her fault—she was just saying what she saw, and I always tell the children they can ask me anything.

In my line of work it's impossible to get five minutes to yourself—even when you're washing. I have to be quick in the shower because it's only a matter of time before there's a little hand knocking at the door, needing my attention.

I have become far too well-acquainted with my bosses' private parts in the past. I'm quite a prudish person, I suppose. I get embarrassed just watching sex scenes at the movies, let alone seeing evidence of my employers' sex lives in the flesh.

The problem is, many actresses have a distorted view of what warrants acceptable behaviour. It's a side effect of the job, as they spend their days filming sex scenes with strangers, baring their bodies to a roomful of film crew. It's not a profession for the bashful.

I've been asked by more than one famous mother to accompany her to a sex shop, usually to choose a present for her husband. I know, I know, we're modern women and it shouldn't be a big deal, but would you be comfortable debating the benefits of one product over another with the person who pays your wages?

I'll never forget the day the mother of a six-year-old girl gave an iPad to her daughter to distract her while we were sitting in a restaurant. She was watching a Disney movie but then got bored and started flicking through the photo album. Our dinner was interrupted by the sound of groaning, and then the six-year-old shrieking. On screen was a video of her mother having sex with the co-star of her latest movie. They were only acting out a scene, thank goodness, but I'm sure it scarred the little girl for life.

I've learnt, over the years, to hide my embarrassment when events like this occur. However, the waxing incident was a new level of intimacy. But I didn't say no, or insist that Alysha leave the room. As I lay with my legs spread, having wax applied to my nether-regions, I wondered how my life had come to this—and how soon I could ask to review my contract. When I'd accepted the job with Alysha I hadn't paid much attention to the clause about 'adhering to the clients' standard of personal aesthetics'. In hindsight, I wish I'd asked a few more questions, as it was too late to complain now.

A mother monitoring their nanny's beauty routine isn't uncommon in A-list circles, where your boss can have an opinion on everything from your weight to your dress sense and hair colour. Some girls spend their twenties changing their looks to please boyfriends, but I'd spent mine morphing into different characters for my clients.

One actress requested that I dye my hair dark brown because she wanted to be the only blonde living in the household. I didn't in the end, but if she'd pushed the issue I would have. She was paying me $450,000 a year. With a salary like that I could afford the best stylist in the country to bleach my hair back again.

It's hard for even the most balanced girl not to get sucked into Hollywood's expectations. This also applied to my dress sense, which had totally changed since I moved to LA. I can now tell the difference between a T-shirt that cost ten dollars and one that has two more zeroes on the price tag. It's unusual for an employer to give you a clothing allowance. Instead, you're supplied with a wardrobe of clothes that are chosen for you. Most mothers don't want you to have your own style in case it isn't to their liking. It's also a strategy to keep the nanny's weight in check. I knew a size-ten nanny whose boss refused to buy her anything but size-eight clothing. That's not a very subtle hint.

That's why I was uneasy, but not totally surprised, about Alysha giving me a head-to-toe makeover. I had expected Will to laugh when I told him, which would help me to make light of the situation, but it seemed I'd misjudged his reaction. 'Lindsay, how can you possibly think that is acceptable behaviour?' he gasped. 'In any other industry your boss would be up before human resources.'

I found myself getting defensive and instantly wished I hadn't told him. 'You don't understand, Will! I live in the vainest town on the planet. Do you know what Alysha has written on her bathroom mirror in lipstick? "Looking good is the best revenge." That's what I have to contend with.'

How could he possibly understand the pressure that I faced living here? Will still lived in Hamilton, where he worked as an accountant, having followed his father into the family business. He still lived two streets down from the house he grew up in, and three nights a week he went back home for dinner. His entire life was based on routine and stability, which wasn't a bad thing, but it couldn't be more different from my own.

'How can you bear to be around people who are that superficial?' Will asked, and I could picture him on the other end of the phone scrunching his eyebrows as he did on the rare occasions he was angry. He was naturally placid, so when he had anything negative to say, the words seemed to get stuck in the pores of his face. It was a trait I always teased him about.

'What do you want me to do, Will? Just quit and come back to Hamilton?' I laughed at the absurdity of this, expecting him to join in, but the comment was met by silence on the other end of the line. 'Oh, come on, Will. You really think one bikini wax is enough for me to turn my back on my life here?'

'Why not?' he exclaimed. 'Come on, Lindsay! When you allow your boss to manage your pubic hair, it could be time to take a good, hard look at your job prospects. There's a great nursery in Hamilton. My sister knows the owner and could probably put in a good word for you. You'd still be able to look after children, but without all this extra nonsense you have to handle at the moment. Wouldn't you like to just do your job, go home at five o'clock and lead a normal life?'

I thought about how I had spent my morning and then I thought about my to-do list for the afternoon. While the children were at a movie screening I had to reorganise their walk-in wardrobe (alphabetically by designer), then pick up a box of bacon cupcakes from the doggie bakery, and then take 9-month-old Chanel to be fitted for her first pair of stilettos. If I had my way the children would spend the afternoon in the park with a bat and ball to occupy them, but I had to follow orders.

The funny thing is, the children would be perfectly happy to live low-key. This is one reason I love caring for the Applebys. The sisters are refreshingly down to earth, in spite of having a mother who I'd once overheard complaining to a girlfriend, 'It's so stressful having more money than I know how to spend.'

In contrast, the Appleby sisters are far more amazed by 'normality' than extravagance. When my Mercedes recently broke down, I was given a courtesy car that didn't have electric windows. Harlow thought the 'wind-down windows' were amazing and turning the handle became her favourite game.

'Okay, it does sometimes feel like my days are taken up with unnecessary—and often ridiculous—tasks,' I admitted to Will, 'But doesn't every job have its downsides? It's just my version of doing admin and dealing with office politics. If I was in a normal job I'm sure I'd still have plenty to complain about.' My best friend didn't answer, but I wasn't sure if that was because I'd won the argument or because my reasoning was so unconvincing that he didn't think it deserved a response.

If I'm honest, there's another reason the thought of getting a 'real job' makes my stomach flip over. It's not because I'd have to take a job with a far smaller salary. It's because I worry that I wouldn't be able to get a job outside the VIP bubble. I may be the go-to girl for celebrities, politicians and royalty, but I wonder if I seem particularly employable to the rest of the population.

I couldn't imagine sitting in a normal interview, being asked about my strengths and weaknesses. I doubted that parents back in Hamilton would value my proudest skill sets. 'I know how to use pepper spray, can recite the Scientology prayer and can spot a paparazzi at twenty paces.'

People in Hollywood have different priorities. I've been asked by a mum during an interview, 'Don't you think my husband looks like Brad Pitt?' as if the wrong answer would put me out of the running.

On another occasion, I went for an interview with a fashion designer who specialised in eco-friendly clothing. The first question she asked me was 'Do you use tampons?' When I answered yes she gave me a lecture on how bad they are for the environment. The next day, I received an email saying I hadn't got the job because of 'Conflicting hygiene morals'.

I once beat six other applicants to a job working for a reality television star because my birthday was only one day apart from hers, which meant that we shared the same star sign. 'We must have compatible personalities,' she trilled. 'Our energies will be in sync.' She didn't even ask to see my CV, which was lucky, because I haven't updated it since I was fourteen years old. I wouldn't know where to start if I had to create a résumé now. Under 'career highlights', what would I list? 'Accompanying parents to waxwork sittings at Madame Tussauds ("Have they made my bum look too big, nanny?")' or 'Applying fake tan to my male boss's (very hairy) body before he appeared on *Dancing with the Stars*'?

I wouldn't even be able to name-drop my ex-employers because I'm bound by a confidentiality agreement not to reveal their identities. So, as much as I sometimes daydreamed about returning to my home town, to sanity and to Will, it just wasn't going to happen. It just wasn't practical.

'Can you please stop saying that?' I huffed at Will. 'It's very easy for you to tell me to quit my job, but my entire life is here. What exactly do I have waiting for me in Hamilton? Really, Will, give me one good incentive. I can't name a single thing that would make it worth going back. Not a thing!'

The telephone suddenly went dead and silence filled the phone booth. I glanced at the display screen, but it said I had $23 left on my phone card. How odd. I tried to call Will back but it went straight to his voicemail.

I felt guilty that our conversation had ended on such a sour note, because I knew that he had my best interests at heart and just wanted me to be happy. I remember, when we were thirteen years old, pricking our fingers and making a blood pact that we'd never live a 'fine' life like most people seemed to. As teenagers we hated the F-word, and banned it from all our conversations. Why settle for fine when you could be amazing?

More than a decade on, I have a feeling that Will thinks I had broken the pact. Honestly, though, I sort of feel like he let me down. I'm constantly trying to persuade him to move to Melbourne to work for one of the big-name accountancy firms, where he could live up to his full potential. Will is the most special person I know—intelligent, funny and not bad-looking if you like that kind of thing. When we were younger, we'd just solve every argument by wrestling. I'm not sure that would go down so well now. The last time I visited Hamilton, we'd had a weird moment where I'd gone to kiss his cheek and he'd twisted his face at the wrong moment. I'm still not quite sure what that meant.

I tried again to redial his number but again it went to voicemail, so I left a message even though I hate the sound of my voice on tape and try to avoid it wherever possible. 'Sorry, Will, I think my phone box cut us off,' I said. 'Look, don't be mad at me. You know you love me, even if I get on your nerves sometimes. I'll send you a picture of my wax job . . . only kidding! Ha ha! Okay, I bet you're not laughing. Well, I better go anyway. I've got to get home to take the baby to ballet and I'm flying to Las Vegas tomorrow because there's a kid's party at Caesars Palace, but I'll call you again this time next week. Hope you have a good one. Love you.'

It's funny, those three words—I love you. Will and I used to say it to each other all the time, but somewhere along the road into adulthood the phrase became too loaded.

I once worked for a famous mother who never, ever told her children she loved them. However, she would throw the L-word around with friends and colleagues. She'd even say it to me every time I left the house or ended a phone call. 'See you later, Lindsay. *I love you!*'

I never wanted to say it back but didn't want to offend her, so instead I'd say 'I love YouTube'. If you say it quickly enough it sounds the same as 'I love you too', but you're not giving your heart away. The truth is, I probably would say those three words to Will. As a friend, I mean. But only if I was sure he'd say them back to me.

4

Every Sunday evening at 6 p.m., you'll find the nannies of Hollywood's wealthiest families at a restaurant just off the Boulevard, where we know our employers will never, ever find us.

It is our official night off but we still feel the need to hide, because our bosses don't really understand the meaning of the phrase 'me time'. If I stayed at home, then Alysha would still give me orders. 'I know you're off duty, but could you just pick up some jars of baby food?' I wouldn't mind if the food was actually for 9-month-old Chanel, but it was Alysha who wanted to eat it. 'The baby food diet worked wonders for Jennifer Aniston,' she had mumbled to me the other day, scooping pureed banana into her mouth from a jar as small as a thimble.

This type of behaviour is exactly why we choose to meet

at In-N-Out Burger. There is no way that our bosses, some of the vainest women on the planet, would ever set foot inside a fast-food joint, in case just the smell of grease instantly brought on an acne attack and made them gain ten pounds.

There are usually between six and ten nannies at our Sunday gatherings. My best nanny friend, Rosie (British, currently working for the blonde actress who always stars opposite the actor with the Southern drawl and six-pack), always saves me a seat next to her at the table. Then there's Opal (a Swedish au pair, working for a troubled pop star) and Mimi (American, whose boss owns half of Silicon Valley). Jess (originally from New Jersey) cares for a six-year-old girl called Rapunzel who has hair down to her waist that is always braided. Her parents, who are fashion designers, remodelled their mansion to look like a medieval castle with turrets and a moat.

The only regular missing from our meeting that night was Nikki, whose fate we discussed in hushed voices. The British nanny just found out she's three months pregnant . . . to the very wealthy, very married businessman she works for. He wanted her to keep the baby, on the proviso that she never, ever revealed he was the daddy. She had to discreetly leave her job, but he was buying her an apartment in Bel-Air and giving her a monthly allowance. This happens more often than you'd imagine, unfortunately, and it gives clean-living nannies a bad reputation.

I honestly don't know how I'd survive without the friendships I've formed with other nannies over the years.

You'd think it would be competitive, as there are so few elite nannies working the circuit, but that's why it's important that we stick together. An outsider can't really understand the demands of our lives.

We are all from different 'nanny tribes', including newborn nannies, travel nannies, day nannies and 'mannies'. It's not unusual for a wealthy parent to employ more than one nanny, even if they only have one child. I am a traditional day nanny, and prefer to work alone because it's far less complicated. However, when I've worked for royalty I'm usually just part of an entourage, and we each have different responsibilities.

The only tribe that doesn't attend our Sunday sessions are the night nannies, who spend the daylight hours sleeping. We probably wouldn't invite them anyway— everybody knows that night nannies are lazy, and their hearts aren't really in it. They choose to work the night shift not because they're naturally nocturnal, but because it's far easier than caring for children during the daytime. You don't have parents watching over you, and your duties are minimal; there's no playing, no cleaning, no homework and you don't have to chauffeur children across the city. A night nanny is paid the same rate as a day nanny for reading a bedtime story, keeping one ear on a baby monitor and rocking a child back to sleep if they wake up. I've worked as a night nanny in the past, but I didn't enjoy it. It's the easiest type of work, but it's also the least fulfilling. Secretly we're pleased that the night nannies can't make it to our Sunday gatherings.

The only honorary non-nanny of the group is Fernando, an Italian make-up artist who I met through Alysha because she hires him for photo shoots and red carpet events. We bonded immediately, as we've worked for many of the same people and can compare stories of bosses from hell. Fernando is wonderfully indiscreet when it comes to his famous clients. We'll flick through a celebrity magazine, and he'll point out his clients. 'She's had a nose job, he paints on his six-pack, and she had her bottom ribs removed to give her that hourglass shape.' He should know, because he's the one in charge of covering every plastic surgery scar.

I'm sure Fernando's clients know that he's a gossip, but he gets away with murder because he's the best in the business. He can make any woman look like Cinderella with a flick of his make-up brush. He is known for being brutally honest and tells clients exactly what he thinks, whether it's criticising their new haircut, their new boyfriend or their latest movie. I'm far too nervous to speak my mind, so Fernando does my dirty work for me. 'Alysha, do you really think dressing a five-year-old in a G-string bikini is appropriate? You may as well get her a garter and a stripper's pole.'

I never get tired of hanging out with Fernando. He would be my ideal man, if he wasn't secretly dating an in-the-closet male model. (You know, the one on the billboards in Times Square, holding a can of soft drink over his private parts. The one currently 'dating' an up-and-coming actress. Yes, that one!)

When I walk into the burger joint, Fernando jumps up from his chair. 'Lindsay-La-La,' he hollers as he envelops me in a bear hug, 'tell me all about your life. What have I missed since I saw you one hundred and sixty-eight hours ago?' He makes me feel like the most special person in the universe every time I see him.

We have a rule that he's not allowed to 'mwah' me. I've worked in this town long enough to know that a Hollywood air kiss is a meaningless greeting, reserved for people you don't really know or don't really like, but need to network with. I want my authentic friends to greet me in an authentic way.

I slumped down into the booth with a sigh, sweeping a handful of Fernando's fries into my mouth before my bum has even landed on the plastic seat. 'Oh, you know, the usual rubbish,' I mumbled through my mouthful. 'I took Chanel to a 5 a.m. baby yoga class, then took seven-year-old Goldie to her ballet rehearsal. Alysha refuses to go because she says the lighting in the dance hall makes her look old. Then I spent the afternoon filling a piñata with twenty-dollar notes for one of the kiddies' birthday parties. I counted about three thousand dollars into that thing. It's totally crazy.'

'That's nothing,' piped up Mimi. 'I have to chaperone Kabbalah summer camp for the next fortnight with over fifty children, one of whom got a prayer bead stuck up her nose. And today my boss told me off because she's decided her five-year-old's skin isn't youthful enough, so now I have to moisturise her face every hour, on the hour. I have to set an alarm so I don't miss an application.'

While Mimi and I traded stories, Opal, who looked utterly exhausted, was anxiously shredding a paper napkin onto the table. She had spent the last week chauffeuring four children back and forth to a rehab facility, where their pop-star mother was currently incarcerated. 'The three-year-old keeps crying because she doesn't recognise her mom,' moaned Opal. 'I've tried to explain that Mommy just shaved her head, but the little girl keeps running away. I'll have to go shopping for a blonde wig tomorrow. The mom's freaking out because her ex-husband wants custody of the kids, even though they're not his biological children and they were only married for 24 hours.'

At this, Fernando broke into a round of applause. 'Opal wins this round!' he cried, 'Congratulations, sweetheart, your boss is officially the most insane.'

It was our favourite Sunday night game, trying to outdo each other's horror stories, although we were always careful to use codenames when it came to our bosses. We secretly referred to Alysha as 'Cake Face', because she wears so much make-up, and Mimi's boss as 'Tupperware Box', because her face is so plastic from surgery and Botox.

We had to keep our voices down, and always chose the booth tucked away in the corner, because it's not unusual for gossip columnists to target groups of nannies to try to unearth juicy stories. It's also not hard to spot a celebrity nanny, if you know what you're looking for. When I'm off duty I usually dress in jeans and a T-shirt, but the clues are in my accessories. At first glance I might look like a university student, but I'm probably wearing a couple of thousand dollars' worth of extras.

For Christmas, Alysha gave me a pair of Chanel studded pumps signed by Karl Lagerfeld. I own six Louis Vuitton bags and seven pairs of Manolo Blahnik stilettos. I have a silver tiara at the back of my closet, which I've only worn once, when I attended a royal gala. When Alysha gave birth to Harlow I was given a 'push present' of a white-gold Chanel watch, despite the fact I wasn't even in the labour suite. I've since had it valued at $16,000, although that doesn't stop me from wearing it when I make sandcastles with the children.

These might seem like generous gestures, but the truth is that many of our employers are on first-name terms with fashion designers. They get more freebies than they know what to do with, and have such short attention spans that they wear an item once and then it's discarded, or re-gifted.

That's why it helps to have the same size feet as your employer. If you happen to be close by when she's throwing away leftovers, you might get lucky. In Alysha's mansion the cleaner vacuums in Prada wedges, the security guards all have Cartier watches, and I've been known to change dirty nappies wearing a diamond ring worth $12,000. Recently Alysha was given a free pair of Gucci sunglasses, wore them once and then threw them away. When I was helping out the housekeepers by taking out the trash I spotted and rescued them, after checking that no one was watching. I'd estimate that, between the five nannies (and one honorary nanny) sitting around the table right now, our accessories alone add up to around $150,000.

I love these girls because they're not lost in show business. They can relate to all my worries and see past the glitz and the glamour. Although we compete for the same jobs, they don't feel like my rivals, and I'm happy to recommend them for work if I think they suit a family better than I do. The other VIP nannies working in Hollywood have become my surrogate family.

There is only one exception—a 26-year-old Australian who I privately call my 'nannemy'. I don't dislike many people, but Madge rubs me up the wrong way. I'm not the only person in our friendship group who has a problem with her. We hoped that, when Kate Middleton announced she was pregnant, Madge would go for the job, but if she did she didn't get it. I would have been happy to have a couple of thousand kilometres between us, but I doubt that Madge will be going anywhere anytime soon. She currently earns $600,000 a year working for a talk show host called Doctor Jaz. It's the show where couples air their dirty laundry with lie detectors and DNA tests. She earns a very generous salary even by elite nanny standards and won't leave that job unless she is forced to. She should be careful, because she will be forced to if Doctor Jaz ever finds out she puts sleeping pills in his ten-year-old son's dinner. 'It's just half a pill to calm him down,' Madge said when she confessed this to us one Sunday. 'The little brat needs to chill out after all those computer games.'

'Watch out! The nannemy has entered the building,' Fernando whispered, gesturing to the restaurant's entrance. As usual Madge was completely overdressed for a burger joint. Today she was wearing a skin-tight Hervé Léger bandage dress that made it laughably difficult for her to squeeze into the booth beside us.

'I'm so, so sorry I'm late,' she gushed. 'I've just left my

new agent!!! We were planning my media strategy!!!' This is how Madge always speaks—in exclamation marks and exaggerations, which makes it very hard to take anything she says seriously.

'Oh, and guess what?' she continued. 'On the way here two fathers asked for my autograph. They recognised me from my movies and wanted childcare advice!!! Isn't that adorable?!!'

To put this into context, by 'movies' she means the five-minute YouTube clips that she films on a webcam and then bullies the fifteen-year-old that she cares for to retouch before she uploads them. It's not exactly primetime television; however, Madge never lets the truth get in the way of a good story.

She is the first to admit she wants to be famous herself, which is the worst trait a VIP nanny can have, as far as I'm concerned. She claims to get 20,000 hits a month on her YouTube channel, but I'm sure most of those are from fathers who couldn't care less about her childcare advice. It's like a webcam show, with Madge pouting and puffing up her breasts for the camera. She posts videos on everything from how to get a child to sleep through the night, to kiddie yoga poses and tried-and-true recipes. Some of her tips are obvious, and some are outright dangerous. When she self-published a fitness book for children it had to be pulled from Amazon and the front cover totally redesigned, because the original had a photograph of a toddler attempting to lift a kettlebell. Fernando was the one to point out that this was a health and safety hazard.

The other thing I dislike most about Madge is that she has no concept of nanny solidarity. She once gave an interview to a magazine in which she claimed that all nannies are home-wreckers who sleep with their bosses. She also once stole a job from my friend Rachael and nearly ruined her reputation. At the time, Rachael was working for a single father whom Madge had a serious crush on and wanted to get close to. One day the dad was emailed a photograph taken on a mobile phone from an anonymous sender. It showed Rachael 'smacking' his two-year-old son when they were at the beach together. The email read, 'Is this the kind of person you want taking care of your child?' The only other adult on the private beach that day had been Madge and, in actual fact, Rachael had been brushing sand off the child's bottom. When Rachael was fired, guess who got the job? That's why I've never said anything about Madge attending our Sunday catch-ups: I'm worried about what she'd do for revenge.

I hate to admit it, but I'm a bit intimidated by Madge. The girl has no volume control, and I find myself growing quieter in her presence to balance out her loudness. Every time I spend time in her company, I leave feeling worse about myself. She has this magical ability to find a person's raw nerve and she goes out of her way to hit it. She once told me her motto is 'There's always a nice way to say something mean.' That says it all, really.

'Lindsay, I was just thinking about you this afternoon,' Madge crowed, swivelling in her seat to face me. My heart sank and Fernando squeezed my knee in solidarity under the table as Madge continued: 'I took the children to watch an episode of Doctor Jaz's talk show being filmed and it was all about fertility. He was talking to girls in their late twenties who thought they had all the time in the world to become mothers. Then they tested their eggs and found out they hardly had *any*. They were *devastated*, as you can imagine.'

I was aware that everyone around the table had puzzled looks on their faces, probably wondering where this conversation was leading. In our group, we never discussed the topic of having babies of our own. When you're a nanny you have to bury your own broodiness, otherwise every day would be like window-shopping when your credit card is maxed out.

'It just reminded me of you for some reason,' continued Madge. 'I think you'd make such a lovely mother. But, as Doctor Jaz said, you're only born with a certain number of eggs and every day the numbers are dwindling. How old are you now? Thirty-four or thirty-five?'

I could have said, 'I'm only twenty-seven years old, thank you.' I could have said, 'I don't even know if I want children.' I could have said a lot of things, but instead I took a huge bite of bacon double cheeseburger so that my mouth was full, and tried not to show that she'd sparked my insecurities.

'Are you okay?' asked Fernando as we left the restaurant an hour later. He had expertly changed the subject by asking Madge about her new Alexander McQueen bracelet, which was a leather band with a gold crystal skull hanging from it. She was all too happy to tell the group how her banker boyfriend bought it for her. Unlike the rest of us,

Madge is not modest when it comes to her accessories and loves to show them off. She is also one of the few nannies who manages to juggle a boyfriend and her career, mainly because she doesn't worry about neglecting the little boy she cares for. The ten-year-old is only too happy to sit in her boyfriend's study playing computer games when he should be at his cello lesson. She bribes him with candy not to tell his father.

'Don't worry about me,' I told Fernando. 'I know she's just trying to hurt me. It doesn't mean anything.' He raised one eyebrow but didn't push the subject, and I went home to lick my paws—and google statistics on fertility.

I tried to push the conversation from my mind, but it wasn't to be. The funny thing about children is they have a magic way of drawing attention to your weaknesses. If you've put on a few pounds, you can bet a little kid will tell you. If you're trying to feign happiness, they'll see straight through you.

The next day I was playing Barbies with Lavender, whose doll collection is so large it has its own bedroom, with an electric train that drives the dolls around a village of houses. 'Let's make a family,' Lavender instructed. 'We can dress up a doll for each of us and have a tea party.' So together we searched through the plastic figurines for a Mummy doll in a tennis costume, a Daddy doll in a director's chair and six tiny dolls to be the sisters.

'Now we need to find a Lindsay doll,' said Lavender, reaching into her toy box and pulling out a figurine. 'This one looks like you . . .'

Of all the dolls, she'd chosen pregnant Barbie complete with a baby bump, wearing a maternity smock. It even came with a tiny blow-up birthing pool.

Either the universe was trying to tell me something, or I needed to lay off the Sunday night hamburgers.

5

Sometimes I feel like I'm trapped in an episode of *Toddlers & Tiaras*, because I've accompanied so many children to auditions, television sets and photo shoots. I've applied fake tan and false eyelashes to five-year-olds and put a toddler in stilettos. Sometimes, when you look around a pageant hall, it's like someone has shot a shrink-ray at a strip joint. I don't enjoy being part of the process but I have to follow the orders of the parents, who are often keen for their children to follow them into the family business.

The three eldest Appleby sisters, Goldie, Harlow and Cherry, had been asked to star in a commercial for a 'healthy' fast food chain where the bean burgers are served in gluten-free buns and the chips are made from sweet potato fried in coconut oil.

The kids were excited because all of the 'talent' who appeared in the advert received a 'milkshake credit card', which bought them unlimited drinks at the restaurant. They'd also be paid, but only Alysha and her agent knew how much and where this money went.

I was glad that the commercial Alysha had signed the girls up to was a group shoot at least. There would be twenty or so children there, so the focus wouldn't be on the Appleby girls. They hadn't even had to audition, because the director played golf with Sir Cameron. This was also how Cherry became the face of a breakfast cereal, how Lavender became an extra in *Glee*, and why little Chanel was appearing in a romantic comedy as Kate Hudson's love child.

You usually see the same children at these types of jobs, and when we arrived at the restaurant where the commercial was being shot I instantly recognised the twin daughters of a country and western singer, and the three sons of a Wimbledon winner.

You can spot a pushy parent from a mile away. At one end of the room, a mother was strapping her five-year-old into a corset while muttering 'This is all your father's fault for giving you that bag of potato chips last month.'

In another corner, a mother was applying a 'tooth flipper' to a little girl's mouth to hide the fact she'd recently been visited by the tooth fairy. I once heard a pageant judge call a three-year-old's tooth gap 'unsightly'. In pageants, girls could also be marked down for having dimples that are 'too symmetrical' or 'over-elongated eyebrows'.

Rosie and Opal were already there with their children,

whose mouths were full of chocolate buttons. To the disgust of the pushy mothers, there is always a 'candy bar' at shoots such as these, with jars full of every American kid's favourite lollies, from cinnamon candy to Hershey's Kisses, Bursting Berry Blow Pops and Tootsie Rolls. These producers are sugar-pushers, because they want to keep the kids' energy levels high (and have sweet treats on hand to bribe the kids with if they don't behave).

Sure enough, when a female crew member wearing a baseball cap with a ponytail swinging from the back rushed up to us, she had a bag of gummy bears in hand and immediately started pouring them into the children's hands. '*Hiya!* I'm Stephanie,' she chirped. 'We're *so glad* that you could join us. Now, I need to get the four of you into hair and make-up *immediately*.'

I gathered Goldie, Harlow and Cherry in front of my legs. 'You mean the three of them,' I said, touching each one on the top of the head. 'We were told the other three sisters were too young to be in the shoot.'

Stephanie looked puzzled for a moment. 'Yes, that's why I said four,' she said slowly. 'You'll need hair and make-up too. We don't want any shiny foreheads, do we? Oh, and can you sign these release forms? Muchos thankyas!'

As she rushed off, she pushed a piece of paper into my hand. At the top of the page it said, 'Name—Lindsay Starwood. Character—Mother.'

My heart sunk. Suddenly my trip to the beauty parlour made even more sense. When Alysha had given me a makeover she wasn't just punishing me for being pap-snapped. She was preparing me to play a Hollywood Mama and needed me to look the part.

While the children were in the make-up trailer having their faces caked with foundation, I called Alysha's agent to get the lowdown. Kerri-Ann was not my favourite person at the best of times, but she would have sealed the deal on my behalf.

'Oh yes, didn't Alysha tell you?' asked Kerri-Ann innocently. 'The casting director wanted a package deal with three children and one parent. Alysha suggested that you take her place, seeing as you have the same hair colour and you've recently lost a bit of weight. I thought you knew. Oh well, break a leg!'

As a large clock in the corner of the restaurant counted down five minutes to action, it was too late to back out. I'd just have to suck it up and pretend to be a mummy.

The children and I were shown to a round melamine table at the centre of the set, a prime position right in front of the main camera. I guessed this was down to Sir Cameron pulling a few strings. The pushy mothers glared at us, wondering why the children were the chosen ones. It probably didn't help that Cherry was loudly and tunelessly singing 'The weebles on the bus go round and round', although I had tried to explain that it was 'wheels'. Meanwhile, Harlow had two bubblegum balls stuck in her cheeks, making her look like a chipmunk. As one mother shoved past me she muttered, 'Who did you sleep with to get this gig?'

The kids and I were given cone-shaped party hats in psychedelic colours with glittering tassels sprouting from the tip to wear. I could understand why Alysha had skipped this job, as she hates to look anything but perfect. A lot of famous mums want their children to appear in commercials, but would never actually lower themselves to that level. I noticed that Opal and Rosie had also been pulled in to play mummies. We rolled our eyes at each other as the crew members fussed about, straightening the kids' outfits and telling them how to place their hands on the tables.

A crew member placed four ice-cream sundaes on the table in front of us, complete with whipped cream, cherries and candles. When the cameras started rolling we had to blow the flames out in unison. Then I had to say my one line: 'I can't *believe* these are sugar-free. Can you, kids?'

This might sound simple in theory, but there were intricate instructions for both the children and me.

'Don't look at the camera, look at your mom,' shrieked the director. 'I want to see a *big* blow of the candle. And *no saliva*! I need a *dry blow*, not a *spray*!'

Blowing out the candles was a fun game for the children the first three or four takes, but the novelty soon wore off as their technique kept being criticised. 'One more time, but don't purse your lips so much, Cherry,' instructed the artistic director; 'One more time, but can you tilt your chin up a little, Goldie?' 'One more time, but could you sit up straighter, Harlow, you've got a little tummy roll going on there.' One more time, one more time, one more time . . .

The children looked more and more confused with each new instruction. I don't think they could understand how a simple activity they did every year at their birthday parties had suddenly become so complicated.

To make things worse, the director clearly hadn't been warned that I was Australian. 'What *is* that accent?' he hollered after my first take. 'This simply *won't* do. We're meant to be an all-American diner.' He turned away and muttered something to an assistant, who frowned and made a note on her clipboard. Stephanie, who had been standing off to the side watching the action, then approached our table to deliver a message.

'The director has requested that you mime your line instead of actually saying the words aloud,' she hissed. 'We're going to have to dub your speech with another actress's voice in post-production. The director wants a voice which is a little more . . . local.'

Maybe I should have been offended, but in a sense I was relieved. At least I didn't have to repeat the line thirty times to perfect the right intonation. It was hard enough getting the candle blowing right, without 'over or under pursing', or 'looking like a fish' as the director had scolded Cherry.

By the time he eventually yelled 'Cut' on our scene we were all out of breath, but our ordeal wasn't yet over. We now had to be extras in a scene where a group of waiters danced across the tables.

'Lindsay, I need the bathroom,' said Cherry, pulling at my arm. She wasn't the only one, as many of the children had been given supersized soft drinks as props and hadn't been allowed a toilet break for an hour. The nannies on set were exchanging nervous glances, knowing that it was only a matter of time before somebody ended up in a puddle.

I tried to signal to Stephanie, but she was too busy taking photos on her mobile, probably posting snaps of our out-takes to the fast food chain's Facebook page. By this stage Cherry was wiggling around in her seat like a performing seal, getting increasingly red in the face. Her mother would kill me if she was caught on camera having an accident.

Then, at the other end of the room I saw Opal scoop up her seven-year-old 'daughter' in her arms and run off the set, scattering crew members.

'*Ewww!*' screamed the little girl who'd been sitting at the same table. 'She *peeed* on *meee*.'

The producer called the shoot to a halt shortly after that. I don't think bodily fluids fitted with his artistic vision. As soon as he yelled 'Cut', every nanny in the room whisked their child into the bathroom. I pulled out a box of baby wipes and rubbed the make-up from the girls' faces. Goldie was already coming out in a rash from the foundation. I was just grateful this was a part-time job for them and not a vocation.

'You were all utterly brilliant today,' I told the girls. 'I was so, so proud of you. You're all little superstars.'

I'm not the kind of nanny who over-compliments kids or showers them with praise—I don't think doing this prepares them for the real world. However, after being around all those pushy parents, I felt the need to overcompensate. The world of junior showbusiness can be cruel and unforgiving.

As we left the diner, I heard one mother lecturing her daughter. 'Why were you smiling so crookedly? I need to speak to your acting coach about this.'

On the drive home, Cherry immediately fell asleep in her car seat, worn out from the bright lights and oxygen expenditure. I was pleased that the other two girls seemed to have enjoyed the experience, not that it's something I'd like them to get too used to.

As we sped down Hollywood Boulevard, Harlow, who was sitting in the back seat, leant forward and tugged my earlobe. 'Lindsay, I liked you being our mommy today,' she said sweetly. 'Are you going to be our mommy from now on? A girl in my class has two mommies and no daddy and my teacher says we're not allowed to tease her. That's the same as our family, right? We have two mommies and no daddy too.'

I didn't know what to say. How could I correct her when, in a strange way, she'd summed up our unorthodox living situation perfectly?

6

Every single evening Alysha gets dressed up and goes out for dinner, despite having a private chef at her beck and call at home. She visits the same three restaurants on rotation, where the cooks have all been schooled on her stringent meal requirements—no gluten, no dairy, no grains and no oils. On top of this, every meal must somehow include coconut. This is because a 'psychic nutritionist' once told Alysha that, in a past life, she'd lived on a coconut plantation, and her 'aura' craved the taste of her homeland. According to Fernando the psychic nutritionist in question has shares in a brand of coconut oil, and that's his standard line to all his wealthy clients.

It doesn't really matter what ingredients are served to Alysha, though, as eating isn't exactly top of her agenda. She only goes to these restaurants to network and to be seen in the right places. Her dining companion is usually a fellow actress, a fashion designer or a director, whose phone number she'll conveniently lose once their careers are on the nosedive.

In the few months that I'd been stationed with the family, Alysha had never once eaten dinner with the children. I had tried to hint to her that it could be beneficial, as I think all families bond best over full bellies, but there was always an important event or companion that prevented her from being at home for dinner. On the upside, I was pleased that the kids weren't being dragged around with their mother every evening. The type of restaurant that Alysha goes to are always overrun with the who's who of Hollywood—usually the most erratic and unstable characters.

I once worked for a famous businessman who would only eat his dinner if he was sitting in a large gold throne positioned at the head of the table. He had a dozen of these thrones, which were delivered to the restaurants that he wanted to dine in so they'd be ready and waiting.

I also worked for an American sitcom star who hated the paparazzi and, when we went out for dinner, would insist on wearing a blanket draped over his head, covering his entire body from scalp to toes. The only part of him you could see was the hand he held his spoon with. It was like eating dinner with Casper the Friendly Ghost.

In Hollywood's most exclusive restaurants, strange behaviour like this is often overlooked, mainly because the craziest celebrities are also the biggest tippers. But these are not the kind of antics I think children should be exposed to, so it's a relief in a sense that Alysha is happy to spend her evenings separately. It's actually my favourite time of the day, sitting down to eat with the kids, without my boss looking over our shoulders.

This is why I was so surprised when Alysha's personal trainer, James, stopped me in the hallway and hissed, 'Hey, Linds, did you get the message about dinner?' I hadn't, but my mind instantly went into overdrive. Was he asking me out? What was I going to say? Was this really a good idea?

I'd be lying if I said I haven't thought about it—James is a former army lieutenant who Alysha met at a charity gala and lured away from active service by naming a salary he couldn't resist. I have on the odd occasion fantasised about wrapping myself around those toned, flexed muscles, but in reality I find James a little intimidating. If we were to date I'd have to constantly hold my stomach in. He'd expect me to be one of those Hollywood robo-mothers who runs marathons eight months in to her pregnancy.

I realised I was getting a little ahead of myself when James broke in to my thoughts by waving his hand in front of my face. 'Earth to Lindsay,' he laughed. 'You looked miles away there for a moment. I was telling you about tonight. Everyone has been told they have to eat out with Alysha . . . and I mean everyone.'

I hadn't got the message, but it didn't seem right. Why would Alysha invite us to dinner? Before I could ask any more questions, the alarm on James's stopwatch sounded. 'Sorry, darling, I've got to run,' he said, 'I've left Alysha in her floatation tank and she'll kill me if her skin wrinkles.'

Then he turned and jogged away down the corridor, as I watched his calf muscles bulging and regretted eating an entire cheese pizza with extra olives the night before.

That afternoon I didn't have much time to dwell on our dinner plans, because Alysha had far more important work for me. Harlow had got a splinter while riding the antique fairground carousel in the back garden and had to have a particular type of pink, glittery Band-Aid. 'I'm sure she'll stop crying if you just kiss it better,' I told Alysha, but instead she instructed me to drive around every pharmacy in Los Angeles until I found somewhere that sold them.

This wild goose chase took me until close to dinnertime. I only remembered my conversation with James when I went back to my bedroom to grab a sweater and found a Diane von Fürstenberg dress bag hanging from my clothes rail. It contained a cream floor-length gown with a long train and flowing sleeves covered in silver sequins. It was stunning, but not exactly child friendly.

There were no instructions, but I knew the drill. If an outfit was left in my room, then it was my cue to put it on. The reason would soon become apparent. I quickly brushed my hair, trying to undo the plaits Harlow had knotted into the back of my head earlier, and brushed some mascara onto my eyelashes. Wherever I was going, that would have to do.

At least I didn't have to waste time worrying about accessories, because Alysha's personal stylist had also laid out shoes and jewellery. As I slid a delicate Marc Jacobs charm bracelet onto my wrist and stepped into a pair of strappy

Jimmy Choos, I thought, 'This would make an amazing date outfit.' It was just a shame that my only plus-ones were under ten years old.

As I tottered down the stairs in all my finery, I was met by a squealing group of children. 'Nanna is here, Nanna is here!' I thought they were talking about me, until I spotted the children's grandmother, Eugenie, walking in the front door, carrying an armful of toys and colouring books. This was odd, as Alysha only invited her mother around if she was desperate for a babysitter, usually on my night off.

'Well, don't you look like a princess,' said Eugenie, as I manoeuvred past the children to kiss her on the cheek. She smelt of buttery toast and Chanel No. 5 perfume, and I suddenly missed my own mum terribly.

I adore Eugenie, a 73-year-old widow who is also a prize-winning novelist, but who lives in a modest studio an hour out of the city. Her gifts to the children are always fun but frugal—bouncy balls, plastic soldiers and packets of M&M's. The kids get more excited by these goody bags than all the elaborate presents their father sends. Last Christmas, after a few too many glasses of eggnog, Eugenie told me it was the worst day of her life when Alysha married Sir Cameron, although she didn't elaborate on the reasons.

'It's so lovely to see you,' I said. 'It feels like it's been ages.' The last time she'd babysat the kids had been the night of the Met Gala, when Alysha's stylist had got a stomach bug and she needed me to act as her 'train manager', to check that the back of her Givenchy gown was in place as she posed for the paparazzi.

'Oh, you know my daughter doesn't like me to intrude into her world,' Eugenie sighed. 'I keep offering to babysit but she says the children's social lives are too busy for their granny. How can a two-year-old even have a social life?'

Although it wasn't my fault, I felt instantly guilty, because I was the one chauffeuring the children here, there and everywhere. 'I'll keep sending photos and drawings,' I told her. 'At least that's better than nothing.'

Unbeknown to Alysha, I send Eugenie care packages containing photos of her growing grandchildren and pictures they drew in art class. Alysha wouldn't let me stick their paintings on her refrigerator anyway, as she said they'd clash with the colour scheme in the kitchen and her interior designer would be offended.

I'm not sure why so many wealthy people distance themselves from their elderly relatives. I once worked for a mother of six who would happily splash out $10,000 on a private-jet trip and $18,000 on a painting but refused to pay for her dying father to have an operation to save his life. I had a sneaky suspicion that Alysha kept Eugenie at a distance because her mother was the only person who knew her real age. She had celebrated her thirtieth birthday for the past two years running, and this year planned to celebrate her twenty-ninth.

As I helped Eugenie wheel her overnight suitcase into the kitchen there was a knock at the door. 'Hey, Lindsay, are you ready to go?' asked Alysha's chauffeur, Seth. 'Everyone else is already waiting at the restaurant.' I kissed the kids goodbye, grabbed my handbag and followed him obediently to the Bentley waiting outside. I wondered which of Alysha's three favourite restaurants I was being taken to. It was always a treat to eat 'adult' food, rather than alphabet spaghetti and vegetables cut into happy faces.

'Well, I won't be eating steak,' I muttered, when we parked outside Minus-47, a raw food restaurant where nothing is cooked above 47 degrees Celsius. Then I gasped out loud, as I spotted Alysha sitting at a table right next to the window. When James had said that 'everyone' was invited to dinner he wasn't kidding. Around the table sat every member of Alysha's entourage, including her three personal trainers, her nutritionist, her masseuse, her hairdresser, her stylist, her agent, her publicist, the chef and even the cleaners. Now I understood why she'd left the children in the care of their grandmother—because there was absolutely no one left to ask.

All of a sudden I'd lost my appetite completely. I had worked for Alysha long enough to know that she must have an agenda for calling us all together. I could tell, even before entering the restaurant, that the atmosphere at the table was awkward. It was messing with the ecosystem, expecting us all to socialise together. It was also messing with some of the staff members' body clocks, as the night watchman would usually just be waking up at this time and James, who got up at 3 a.m., would usually be going to bed.

'Oh, Lindsay, you're here,' Alysha gushed as I neared the table. 'Isn't it just fabulous that everybody could make it on this special night? I'm so glad that we could all get together as a family.'

Her publicist and agent seemed less than impressed by this statement, and I bit back my laughter. In the hierarchy of hired help, Alysha's office staff considered themselves above the rest of us. They count themselves as professionals and the rest of us as mere servants. I found this funny, as I happen to know that I'm paid more than both her publicist and agent put together.

When I moved in with my first celebrity family, I used to hate living in a house with such a large team of staff, because I wasn't used to people picking up after me. It felt indulgent to have cleaners sweeping my bedroom, laundresses washing my clothes and drivers transporting me everywhere. It felt especially ridiculous being chauffeur-driven to the school pick-up. Why was my presence even necessary when there was an adult already driving the vehicle?

But over time I've learnt that everyone has a unique role and it's best just to go along with it. I don't think I'm above any other member of staff, and I think it's important we all stick together. That's why I learnt Spanish, because it's the first language of many of the household staff. It means we can talk about our bosses without them knowing, which is why I learnt all the swear words first.

As Alysha continued to talk, I mouthed one of these words across the table at her housekeeper, who laughed and rolled her eyes at the ridiculousness of the situation.

'I'd like to thank you all for coming to this celebration,' Alysha continued, as if we'd had a choice. 'I have very, very big news. We're all going to be *reality television stars*! Well, the children and I are. You'll be more like extras . . . but isn't that still exciting for all of us?'

Now I understood the motivation for this dinner. She'd bought us here to butter us up, and had chosen a public place so that we couldn't cause a scene. I noticed that beside every dinner plate there was a thick cream envelope, which was stamped with the logo of a production company.

'Now, there's just a teeny tiny bit of paperwork,' said Alysha. 'The producer needs everyone to sign a contract. It's all very straightforward and is nothing for you to worry about. You probably don't even need to read it . . . it's probably a little too complicated for you all. You just need to sign it by the end of dessert.' She then signalled the waiter. 'Anyone for Champagne? Now, don't say no, or I'll be offended. It's a celebration, after all.'

At first nobody reached for their envelope, even though we were clearly all itching to. It's like the first rule of going to a glitzy celebrity party—never *ever* look inside the goody bag until you're out of public view. It's not the done thing to show excitement over freebies. So, as Alysha doled out the champagne and pushed morsels of food around on her plate, I discreetly slipped my envelope into my handbag and excused myself to go to the bathroom.

I only peeled open the package once I was safely inside a toilet stall. I would like to say it was shocking, but after a decade working around showbusiness, it was, unfortunately, exactly what I expected. As well as asking for permission to use my image 'as the producer sees fit', it stated that 'The producer has the right to edit, delete and fictionalize the footage at his or her discretion.' In signing the contract I was also indicating I understood that 'it may expose you to public ridicule, humiliation or condemnation.' Yeowch! They really weren't pulling any punches.

I'm not sure what was worse—being treated like a second-class citizen, or being treated like one of the family and dragged into Alysha's fame game.

•

The next morning I woke up feeling exhausted and tearful. I blamed the Champagne I'd drunk the night before. Alysha had insisted on topping up our glasses, and hadn't allowed us to leave the restaurant until we finished the five bottles.

'Oh, don't worry, Champagne doesn't give you a hangover,' she trilled. 'I'm always perfectly capable of functioning the next morning, even when I've drunk far too much.'

I didn't want to point out that Alysha's average day involved waking up at noon, having a facial and then meeting her agent for a liquid lunch at The Ivy. She would probably feel the side effects of alcohol if she had a screaming child to bath, or a kitchen floor to scrub. I don't think a hangover is a problem experienced by the upper classes.

It's days like this when I wished I didn't live with my employers. I know, I shouldn't complain when my accommodation, food and even my toiletries are paid for. I don't like complaining about my job, because I know I'm very lucky, but everyone has a bad day at the office sometimes and Alysha's announcement had left me feeling anxious.

I had a feeling that her new reality television career would come back to bite us all.

Unfortunately, I didn't have the luxury of sitting around feeling sorry for myself. I had to shake myself out of my slump because I had a big day ahead of me, including taking Goldie to a music concert that evening. A seven-year-old in her class had just released an album, which was currently rising up the charts, although I thought the lyrics were a little explicit for a schoolgirl. She was the third girl in Goldie's class to sign a recording contract. Their end-of-year play was like a live episode of *Glee*.

In a few hours I would be front and centre stage at a concert, surrounded by hyperactive schoolgirls, so I needed to snap out of my hangover and stop moping around. I fell back on a strategy I use whenever I'm feeling blue—I just think about the worst boss I've ever had, which always puts my current troubles into perspective.

Every VIP nanny has a story about a boss from hell who made their life miserable. In my case, it wasn't actually a parent, but the new girlfriend of a father who I worked for. Remember Steven Stavros, the unfaithful pop star? He eventually left his wife Barbie after falling in love with a Canadian model he met on Facebook. He had shared custody of his kids, who were teenagers by this point, and asked me to move back in temporarily to help them adjust to the newly fractured family.

He also moved in his new girlfriend, Jamie, who was clearly determined to prove she was the new head of the family. The model-turned-fashion designer had a reputation for being a diva. She had already been married four times and sold the photos from her last wedding to a magazine for a cool $3 million. She was used to getting her own way and clearly didn't like that my relationship with Steven verged on being a friendship rather than just a professional acquaintance.

One morning Steven came back from a gym session and I casually asked, 'How did you like the new trainer? Did he put you through your paces?' She spun on her heels and barked, 'That is no way for a staff member to talk to their employer. How *dare* you speak to him like that?!'

As punishment for my error of judgement she then instituted a rule that I was no longer allowed to speak to Steven directly, or even make eye contact with him. It sounds unbelievable, but if I wanted to say hello to him, I had to tell Jamie and she would pass on the greeting. I hoped that Steven would stick up for me, seeing as we'd known each other for years, but he seemed to be under her spell. Even the kids had picked up on the fact that their dad had suddenly started dressing differently, had lost weight and had a suspiciously smooth face. Jamie visited a beautician every single day for some treatment or another, and Steven had started going with her.

That wasn't the only thing that changed. The kids weren't allowed to call me Lindsay anymore. They were told to refer to me only as 'nanny'. I also wasn't allowed to make direct eye contact with Jamie or any of her friends. After three months in the job I found myself automatically stooping and had to see an osteopath to correct my neck ache.

If you think this is unfair practice, some nannies I know have even more extreme stories. I've seen a mother slap a nanny in the face in the first class lounge of an airport because she'd forgotten to pack the children's favourite bubblegum-flavoured toothpaste.

Another nanny I know, who worked for an Indonesian billionaire, was never allowed to use the same toilet as the family or drink out of the same glasses. A nanny who I met in India was made to sleep in a storage room under the stairs, despite the fact the mansion had sixteen spare bedrooms.

In comparison to some of these living conditions, working for Alysha didn't seem so terrible. It's hard to wake up on the wrong side of the bed when you're falling asleep in the lap of luxury. My bedroom in the Appleby mansion has a four-poster bed with a $50,000 cashmere mattress, made by the company that supplies beds to the British royal family. All of Alysha's staff are given matching silk pyjamas monogrammed with the Appleby crest. We're banned from sleeping in anything else in case there's a fire and we have to evacuate. God forbid we weren't colour coordinated for the fire brigade.

It wasn't exactly ideal that my bed would soon have a television camera installed over it, but it was something I was going to have to learn to live with. According to the contract laid out by the production company, none of the rooms of the house would be off-limits, including the staff quarters and their ensuites. They had insisted that cameras would be placed at a 'modesty-preserving angle'. I'd just have to start getting changed in my closet.

I'm used to being watched, although it's usually not by two million viewers. In wealthy homes you're never out of sight of a security camera, security guard or night watchman. This means you can never let your guard down and have to be professional at all times. The cameras even have night vision.

I was caught out in the early days of my career, before I realised that an eye-in-the-sky was always watching me. As a sixteen-year-old, working for the Shawshanks, I used to dance while I vacuumed, pretending that I was Mrs Doubtfire. I even put on a Scottish accent and used to really get into character. I didn't realise that Jason Shawshank had the security footage streamed directly to his laptop.

I only found out, one evening at a party they held at their mansion, when 'Dude (Looks like a Lady)' came on the stereo and he started mimicking my dance moves. I'm lucky that he had a good sense of humour and it became a long-running joke between us.

I didn't think Alysha would find it as amusing if I was seen to be mixing business with pleasure. It would be the equivalent of the policeman who was caught doing a cartwheel during the royal wedding.

As I dressed Goldie in the outfit that she wanted to wear to the concert—a pink Chanel tutu and a T-shirt printed with a photo of her pop star friend—I thought about how many people would kill for the opportunity she'd had. I once worked for a judge on *The X Factor*, and have seen firsthand the lines of auditionees who queue around the block, desperately hoping for their fifteen minutes of fame.

I don't have any such ambitions. I might live underneath the bright lights of Hollywood but being a celebrity nanny isn't a stepping-stone to fame—in fact, it will more likely put you off ever entering the spotlight.

I see the downsides of stardom every day, from the loss of privacy, to the bad reviews and even death threats. I see actresses sobbing over their piles of hate mail. (If they say they don't read them, don't believe them.)

My bosses may seem like show-offs, but I see signs of their insecurity. Next to Alysha's bed is a pile of self-help books with titles such as *Dealing with Loneliness* and *How to Find Your True Life's Purpose*.

As I sprayed Goldie's hair with glitter, she sang into her hairbrush. 'Goldie, would you like to be a pop star?' I asked her. 'Would you like to be on stage in front of all those people, like your friend?'

My seven-year-old charge looked up at me with a disparaging expression. 'Why would I want to be up there?' she asked. 'She's up there on her own. I want to be dancing with the people below.' I couldn't help smiling with pride.

7

'Is the circus here?' asked Lavender, peering out of her bedroom window. I could understand her confusion. With three trucks, seven trailers and a marquee in the driveway, it did look as if the circus had come to their garden.

The Appleby house had been thrown into complete chaos thanks to the arrival of the reality television film crew, who were now permanently living in the courtyard. A team of twenty men worked in shifts, eating and sleeping in trailers when they were off duty. There was never a moment when a camera wasn't rolling and there was a constant stream of crew members crashing through the house at all hours of the day and night.

On top of this, cameras had been installed in all of the light fittings, which were constantly whirring overhead, and red lights flickered in all of the pot plants. Alysha had also ordered fifty full-length mirrors, which were installed on every wall in the house, to ensure she could check her appearance at all times. It felt like I was being trapped in a giant changing room, with reflective surfaces everywhere you looked. It also meant the last shred of privacy I had was taken away.

I usually have breakfast at 4 a.m., because it's the only time of the day I can let my guard down. Alysha rarely wakes before midday and the night nanny is on call until 4.30 a.m., so it's usually my only moment to myself. However, as I discovered on the second day of filming, there is no downtime in reality television.

As I tiptoed into the kitchen wearing the clothes I'd slept in—skimpy shorts and a singlet (my monogrammed pyjamas were in the wash)—I collided with a burly, bearded crew member, carrying a lasso of electrical cords over his shoulder. 'Well, good morning,' he chuckled, as I glanced down to check how revealing my top was and found it was worse than I feared.

'Umm, good morning,' I replied, not wanting to appear rude. To cover my embarrassment I opened the fridge and buried my head in the top shelf, pretending to look for something. 'Where's that orange juice?' I muttered. The bottle was right in front of me, but I needed time to compose myself.

I could hear the technician chuckling behind me and wondered what was so funny. Then I heard the buzz of a walkie-talkie. 'Testing, testing,' he said. 'Is that picture clear enough for you, boys?'

That's when I spotted a flashing red light coming from

behind a pot of coconut yoghurt. I couldn't believe it. They'd hidden a camera inside the fridge, looking outwards at chest height. This meant that, as I bent over, a crew member in a trailer somewhere was getting an eyeful, right down my top. I glared at the camera, before grabbing an apple and retreating to the safety of my bedroom.

I couldn't really complain seeing as I'd signed the production company's contract, which had included the statement, 'This show may include scenes of nudity, sex and violence.' Also, I wasn't really worried that my nipple flash would make the final cut. My modest assets weren't the stars of the show, or even impressive extras, as Cherry had recently pointed out to me when I'd taken her to a swimming lesson. 'Lindsay, your boobies aren't nearly as big as Mommy's,' she'd pointed out helpfully, in front of ten other children and their nannies. Thank you, Cherry. Obviously, Alysha didn't have to worry that my breasts would steal her attention.

'I hear you got caught on "cleavage cam" this morning,' laughed Fernando, when our paths crossed in the hallway later that morning. He was on his way to give Alysha a vajazzle and I was taking Goldie to her web design class. This was the trendiest extracurricular activity among Hollywood kids, as every parent wanted their child to be the next Mark Zuckerberg—with better dress sense, of course.

The plus side of having a crew permanently at the house was that Fernando had been asked to work for Alysha full time, as she needed constant hair and make-up.

He was now there from 6 a.m. to 11 p.m. every day and on call during the night for 'cosmetic emergencies'. I couldn't be happier about having an ally nearby, especially as Fernando still spoke his mind even when the cameras were rolling.

He was the only staff member who had refused to sign the consent form, which meant his face had to be blurred when he was in a shot, like a criminal in *Cops*. 'It makes me seem mysterious,' he explained, 'plus I don't give away my talents for free. If they want me that badly, they can give me my own show, baby!'

If it was anyone else, I suspect they'd be fired, but as usual Fernando lived by his own rules and everyone else had to work around him.

Alysha was certainly taking her reality television role very seriously. She even had a director's chair especially made with her name splashed across the back in big, glittery letters. She also changed her outfit up to seven times a day to keep her look 'fresh'. Her stylist had her work cut out, begging designers from across the world to lend Alysha free outfits.

As well as the film crew, make-up team, a stylist and all their assistants, who seemed to spend their days drinking Diet Coke and dropping their cigarettes in the fountain, a team of six lawyers were also living at the house.

Alysha was taking no chances with how she was represented and the lawyers were assessing every snapshot of footage. The other day I'd heard one poor cameraman being scolded for filming Alysha eating a stick of celery.

Instantly, a lawyer appeared out of nowhere. 'Do I need to remind you of clause 23 of the contract?' she hissed. 'My client is never, ever to be filmed eating.' It was all I could do not to let out a giggle. Alysha's pet hate is the sound of other people chewing, and it would be her worst nightmare to be filmed with her mouth full.

There were cue cards posted around the house with reminders such as 'chin up' and 'hover off the chair'. The last order was from Alysha's stylist. 'When you sit on a chair it makes your thighs spread out,' she warned. 'Can you try and just hover about a centimetre off the seat?'

I decided pretty quickly that any reality star who says their show isn't staged is lying. Even if other shows are only half as stage-managed as Alysha's, that still means there's a fair amount of fakery involved. They tell certain people to make certain comments; they set up phone calls and scenarios where you 'bump into' long-lost friends and relatives. Some of these relatives aren't even really related to the star but are actors hired to play a part.

'Do you know that my daddy has stick-on hair?' The conversation around the kitchen table halted as Cherry made her announcement without even looking up from her colouring book.

Alysha and her producer had been debating whether or not a film crew should be sent to India, where Sir Cameron was currently working. So far, the only cameo he'd made in the show was a two-minute Skype conversation, where he'd said 'Hello' and then the screen had frozen. He didn't seem keen to take part and had even banned the film crew from stepping into his study, which only made them more keen to do so.

'It will seem more real if he appears in the show,' argued the producer. 'Otherwise it might look like you're hiding something and viewers will grow suspicious.'

That's when Cherry had decided to pipe up with her revelation about her daddy. Luckily, she was distracted when her red crayon snapped in half (hashtag 'preschool problems') and the adults quickly glossed over the subject and moved on.

I didn't blame Sir Cameron for setting boundaries to protect his privacy. I was actually surprised that Alysha was letting a television crew inside her real home, instead of renting another property to film in. When a celebrity is photographed 'at home' it often isn't really where they live at all. A lot of reality television stars just hire a mansion, put some family photos on the mantelpiece, move the pets in and pretend they've lived there for years—despite the fact their kids don't know the way to the bathroom.

It seems like lying comes second nature to some starlets, who are so desperate to impress that they fabricate entire layers of their lives. I know one wealthy housewife who is a notorious storyteller. She told all her friends that she was an *FHM* model. When they asked why none of her photos were on the internet, she claimed her husband had them all taken down. She also claimed to have ordered five Bentleys, which were mysteriously never delivered, and that she had been an Olympic downhill skier. The clincher was when she said *the* Molton Brown was coming to her Molton Brown–themed birthday party . . . until someone pointed out that Molton Brown is not actually a person, just a product name.

However, Alysha had decided she wanted to be 'authentic' and allow cameras into her real home. This was funny because in every other area of her life she was happy to fake it. I happened to know that her new Chanel handbag was hired at a cost of $1000 a week, because she couldn't get to the top of the waiting list to buy one. She had fake hair, fake eyelashes and fake nails; even her age was fake.

She'd even hired a 'social media ghostwriter' who now updated her Facebook, Twitter and Instagram feeds for her. I felt sorry for Alysha's fans who were excited to get a reply from a soap star, not realising that it wasn't actually her writing back to them. Instead, Alysha's social media accounts were managed by a 25-year-old technology graduate called Crystal, who had turned down a job with NASA to work with Alysha. 'It's only for a year until I pay off my student loan,' Crystal told me. 'You wouldn't believe how much I get paid for writing a few Facebook posts.' She's previously handled the Twitter account of an actress from *Gossip Girl*, so she was used to tweeting like a celebrity.

It really is amazing how much of your life can be outsourced when you have an unlimited budget at your disposal.

I was just thankful that the children were being kept relatively out of the pantomime and hadn't been included in any of the scripted scenes. They were more like extras than cast members and were filmed running around in the background, but weren't the focus of the film crew's attention.

'You might face a backlash if the kids are too involved,' I'd overheard Alysha's lawyer warning her. 'You won't come off favourably if you're seen as exploiting them for ratings.' Alysha knew this was true, as she was friends with a British model who'd come under fire for putting her children at the centre of a reality TV show. She didn't want to risk the same criticism.

I'd been told to keep the children out of the house as much as possible between 3 and 6 p.m., the time when the sunlight was the most flattering for filming. This wasn't hard because the children's social calendars were busier than Paris Hilton's in the nineties, with afterschool clubs, birthday parties and press events to attend. They were on the VIP list for the opening of every toy store, junior sample sale and kids-movie premiere in the city. I had to set up an online calendar for each of them just to keep track of where they should be and, as their surrogate parent, I also had to attend all of the activities. In Hollywood, even the baby classes where adults sit in a circle and sing nursery rhymes tunelessly with their babies in their laps are often called 'Nanny and me' rather than 'Mommy and me'.

The children never really complained about their schedules, because they didn't know any different, and all of their school friends were equally busy. However, I constantly felt guilty as I shipped them between appointments. I think young children need rest, structure and stability, not press conferences and photo opportunities.

I do not think it's healthy, on a Tuesday evening, to chauffeur a six-year-old straight from school to a hair salon to have an 'up-do' before a charity fundraiser. However, try telling this to Alysha, who is determined that one of her children will be mentioned in *TIME* magazine's list of the '50 youngest philanthropists in America'.

As well as late-night events there were also early-morning gatherings. Every day, on the way to school, I had to stop off at Starbucks. This was a ritual shared by all of the girls' classmates, who each had Starbucks credit cards they could just swipe at the counter. 'It will make them more alert for their lessons,' explained Alysha, although I put my foot down when it came to giving them caffeine. Currently, the fashionable drink for schoolgirls was a babycino made with frothed almond milk and sweetened with agave nectar. It was a bizarre sight, seeing a cafe full of children chugging down their 'coffee'. Many of them looked as tired and stressed out as businessmen.

I could tell the constant presence of the reality film crew was taking its toll on Goldie when one morning she asked me to supersize her Starbucks order. The previous evening she'd had a triple-whammy of activities, going to pony club, then an etiquette lesson and then a yoga class, and hadn't got home until midnight.

As we queued at the counter she pulled at my shirtsleeve and looked at me with wide eyes. 'Lindsay, I just don't think I can *function* unless I have an espresso *pronto*,' she cried dramatically. 'And *pleeease* can you make it a double'. I was having a deja vu moment, as her mother had barked the exact same order at me the morning before. It's amazing how impressionable kids are at that age.

'Do you actually know what an espresso is, sweetie?' I asked gently. 'It's a drink for grown-ups and will probably make your tummy feel sore.'

She stared at me as if I was keeping something from her. 'But Mommy says it's magic,' she said questioningly. 'When she's grumpy she just needs to drink out of one of her teeny tiny cups and she's happy again, and doesn't even need to eat lunch.'

At this moment I could have attempted to explain the science behind caffeine, but I doubted Goldie would understand it until she was a few years older. Instead I opted for the nanny's last resort—a little white lie. When we got to the counter I ordered Goldie a babycino but asked for it in an espresso cup, to fool her. After one sip she perked up instantly and began bouncing around the room, bumping her cup against her classmates, and saying 'Cheers' in a fake British accent.

I felt guilty that I had indulged her with a placebo, but it could have been worse. As we left the cafe, one of Goldie's school friends was standing outside sucking on a lollypop stick. Her mother was barking into her mobile phone, with a cigarette hanging from her fingertips.

•

I make it my mission to try to inject some normality into the kids' lives—although this can be easier said than done at times. They spend so much time around adults, participating in age-inappropriate activities, that I see it as part of my job to balance it out. How do children outside the Hollywood bubble enjoy themselves? What does their playtime look like?

The problem is that, even when I try to engage the kids in low-income fun, it somehow always ends up with a Hollywood twist. The day we set up a lemonade stall was the perfect example.

'When I was a little girl I used to sell homemade lemonade from the end of my parents' driveway every weekend,' I told the little girls as we squeezed lemons into crystal jugs (Alysha doesn't allow plastic crockery in the house, as she has a phobia of picnics. Really. She says there's no way to sit flatteringly on a picnic rug). I was pretty pleased with myself for coming up with the Sunday activity. I had visions of the girls handing out lemonade cups to people in passing cars in exchange for fifty cent coins. It would be a lesson in the value of money, and the fun that can be had when you work hard.

I'd been to the market that morning and bought a huge tub of lemons, smuggling in a bag of sugar—the white stuff is forbidden in this household. Alysha spent every Sunday morning cocooned in a full-body detox wrap in her bathroom (her ensuite has a sauna, sunbed and oxygen chamber in it). I hoped that would keep her busy until we'd mixed up the sugary cocktail. Unfortunately we were delayed after Cherry squirted lemon juice in her eye and I had to make her a pirate's eye patch out of the back of a cereal box to cover it. She didn't actually need it; her eye was fine, but she'd never miss any excuse to get dressed up.

Of course, the fancy dress sesh soon spiralled. Goldie wanted to wear her Ninja Turtle costume, and Lavender screeched for her Elmo bodysuit (a genuine Sesame Street costume used on the show that Alysha had bought for $3400 at an auction). The other children opted for their tried-and-tested onesies.

'Right, little ones, let's hit the road,' I said, when we were suited and booted. At Cherry's request I was wearing a Pippi Longstocking outfit, with a wig that had long, stiff plaits that stuck out the sides of my head. Move over, Daphne Guinness!

As our gang of characters headed back into the kitchen I was greeted by the sight of my boss, still wrapped in her detox mask, which had hardened to a green shell. I'm not even sure how she'd got herself into an upright position, seeing as she didn't seem able to bend her knees or elbows.

'Mommy, are you playing dress-up too?' cried Cherry, excited by the rare opportunity to actually play with a parent. Alysha ignored her. I saw her eyes—the only part of her visible beneath the bandages—flick in my direction. 'Lindsay, what the hell is going on here?' she exclaimed, 'Why do my children look like they've just escaped from a mental asylum?'

I gestured to the pile of lemons. 'We're going to have a lemonade stand outside the front of the house,' I explained. 'I thought it would be a good . . . teaching opportunity.'

I can never predict how my boss will react to certain situations. When I'm sure she'll fly off the handle she often stays calm, and when there's really no reason to be tricky, she can turn into King Kong. I once tried to map her mood swings on an iPhone app, but even a high-tech algorithm couldn't find a pattern.

If I could have seen her face beneath the detox mask, I'm guessing she'd have looked thoughtful. When she eventually answered she surprised me. 'That's a *fantastic* idea,' she cried. 'It's just the kind of wholesome content we need for the reality show.'

Of course, the show. It was all about the show. Obviously. But at least she hadn't put a blanket ban on the activity. 'Sounds good, Alysha,' I replied. 'I'm just going to grab a wooden crate from the garage to use as a table and then we'll be ready to go.'

I should have known it was too good to be true. Alysha's idea of wholesome fun was a little more high-end than I'd envisioned. 'Oh no, that won't do,' she said. 'I'll give Tilly a call. She can design a lemonade stand for you.' Tilly was Alysha's interior decorator, who was as much a permanent feature of the house as the furniture she had purchased. The Appleby household was like her Golden Gate Bridge—as soon as one level was redecorated, she started all over again.

'That's a very kind offer, but I don't think it's really necessary.' I tried to be as polite as possible. 'All we need is somewhere to rest the lemonade jugs. I can just lay a tablecloth over the box. It's what I always did when I was a little girl.'

I realised too late that I shouldn't have mentioned my own childhood, as it just acted as a benchmark for Alysha to upstage. 'Oh but, Lindsay, this isn't some wilderness town in *Australia*,' she said. 'This is Hollywood. We have slightly higher standards. Do you really think cars here will stop at a box by the side of the road?' Well, yes I did, when that box had six adorable children standing next to it. But you have to choose which battles to fight in my game, and this wasn't one of them.

The children were rightfully disappointed when I had to explain that we, sadly, wouldn't be playing lemonade stand today, because we needed to wait a week for a stall to be designed and constructed so that we didn't bring down the tone of the neighbourhood. I appeased them by freezing the homemade lemonade into sorbet, which we guzzled in front of the TV that evening. It also meant that, by the following Sunday, they were more excited than ever.

As for the lemonade stand, well, Tilly had certainly gone all out. Although that might have been because she charged $450 per hour. She'd built a mini cafe facade with an oak wood frame and a white-and-red striped canopy. It had a vintage lemonade dispenser, like you'd see in an old sixties diner. She'd even found—or custom-made—a neon sign that read 'Pop Stop' and ran on a generator that was also connected to a bubble machine. The lemonade stand looked like it belonged in Disneyland, especially when it was manned by six kids in fancy dress outfits.

The TV producer had dispatched a cameraman to hover around us. He didn't seem too pleased that he had to video our entrepreneurial escapades rather than watching the Dodgers game the rest of the crew were glued to in their trailer. But he soon perked up when our first customer arrived, ten minutes later. As the Jaguar with the blacked-out windows slowed down and pulled over at the side of the road, the children jumped up and down excitedly. Phew! I'd had a secret fear that nobody would stop for them. We'd set the price per glass at $1.50, but famous people can be ridiculously frugal when it comes to opening their wallets. It's partly because they get so much given to them for free and partly because they rarely carry cash, particularly loose change. If it's not a hundred dollar bill, it's not worth anything to them.

The sun was shining in my eyes, so I didn't clock our customer's face until he was directly in front of the lemonade stand. I faked a cough to hide my gasp. It was James Bond! Not that he was in character, of course, but it was one of the actors who had played him. (I won't say who, but let's just say he's my favourite Bond of them all.) The children were totally clueless as to the identity of their star customer. They were just excited to be given attention.

'You should have two glasses. No, have three. Have four!' sang Harlow, thrusting empty plastic cups into the hands of the Oscar winner.

'Hang on, girls,' I stepped in before she could hand over the whole packet of cups. 'The gentleman probably just wants one glass. He probably isn't that thirsty.' But I had underestimated the power of a seven-year-old with puppy dog eyes, as Harlow stared up at her customer. 'But it tastes like sunshine,' she bleated, 'and we made it all by ourselves . . .' Wow, this girl knew how to do the hard sell.

'Well, in that case, how can I refuse?' I was amazed when Bond (sorry, that's how I'll always think of him) pulled his wallet from his pocket and took out a stack of notes. 'How much for an entire jug? Or how about a hundred dollars for the whole lot?'

The girls were over the moon. A part of me wanted to protest. It seemed like easy money for barely any work. Wasn't I meant to be teaching them the satisfaction of toil and struggle? *Oh well*, I consoled myself, *maybe it's just a different lesson, on the generosity of strangers.*

As 007 drove away balancing the jug between his knees ('I'm a neighbour so I don't have far to go. Don't worry!') I was just thankful I'd bitten my tongue and not made a 'shaken not stirred' reference. Alysha would have killed me if that had been caught on camera. The cameraman had perked up considerably. 'Well, that was a good cameo,' he laughed. 'That's a wrap. I'm going back to the trailer. You're not going to top that customer.'

That evening, as I watched Harlow squeeze the hundred dollar note through the slot in her piggy box (she'd decided to keep it 'safe' for her sisters), I thought back to my own childhood, when Will and I would run our own lemonade stand. The most we ever made in a day was $19.65 and we were over the moon, counting silver coins into one-dollar piles. This was a different world, and maybe I just had to accept that. A world where interior decorators design lemonade stalls and 007 makes it a sell-out.

The girls had decided that next time they wanted to sell cupcakes instead. I made a mental note to start practising my red velvet recipe in case Martha Stewart happened to drive by.

•

'Will, it's me,' I squealed excitedly into the phone.

It's a silly thing, but I always get a warm feeling when I call Will and say 'It's me'. I love having someone in my life who recognises my voice immediately.

'Look, I know you're in the office but I just had to call you. I've had *such* a fun day. Wait until I tell you who I met . . .'

There was silence on the other end of the line. Clearly my excitement wasn't being reciprocated. When Will finally did answer he sounded impatient. 'Lindsay . . . look, I'm a little busy right now. Can I call you back later? I'm right in the middle of something.'

What? I was taken aback. Will was never too busy to talk to me. Granted, it was Monday morning in Hamilton, but I'd been to his office. We're talking a small country accountancy firm—it's not exactly the New York Stock Exchange. There's a reason they have a ping-pong table in the back room and their pot plants always die from being overwatered.

I wanted to spill my exciting news to him like I would have when we were kids, but I had to be an adult and appreciate he had responsibilities. I wasn't going to let Will know how rejected I felt. 'Sure, sure, babe,' I quipped. Then I instantly regretted my choice of words. Will and I do not have a 'babe' type of relationship and to him it would sound like such an Americanism.

'I mean, sure *Will*,' I corrected myself quickly. 'Shall I call you in an hour? Or later tonight after I put the kids to bed?' Bedtime for the girls would be late afternoon in Hamilton. I knew that a lot of people in Will's office only worked part-time and left in the afternoon to pick up their kids from school, so I thought he might be grateful for some long-distance company.

'I'm actually pretty busy all day, and I have plans tonight so I need to leave on time.' He sounded sheepish. 'Can I call you when I have some free time? Maybe over the weekend?'

In any other friendship this wouldn't be a big ask, but there are reasons I always call Will and not the other way around. Number one, I have to go to a pay phone for privacy. Number two, my schedule is insane, so the chances are if he called me I probably wouldn't be free.

I started to explain this to Will (for the hundredth time) while trying not to sound too self-important. He let out a disgruntled sigh. 'We're *both* busy people, Lindsay. I have a career too, you know, and a life to try and maintain outside the office. Look, can you at least set up a Facebook account so we can send instant messages?'

This wasn't the first time he'd raised the Facebook topic, and my response was always the same. 'You know I'm not allowed a Facebook account, Will,' I sighed. 'If my boss found out I was on social media she would fire me.'

It might sound extreme because of Alysha's carefully managed presence on social media, but she banned anyone else in the household from even having a Facebook account—her children and staff members. This is very common rule set by parents in the spotlight. They fear their children will be targeted by trolls and pestered by reporters if they have an online presence. It's a hard ban to enforce with older children, and I've heard of nannies helping teenagers set up pseudonymous Facebook accounts using their real first name and a fake surname created by typing their actual surname in to a thesaurus (guess who Jonas Voyage is?).

It's also a matter of security, especially if I'm working for a member of a royal family or a high-profile politician, whose children could be targeted by kidnappers.

The frightening reality is that it's not hard to hack into someone's Facebook page and use it to track their location. A friend of mine worked for the White House and got into serious trouble for 'checking in' to Air Force One on Facebook with their exact location over the Indian Ocean.

It had been a topic of dispute between Will and me on more than one occasion. 'I can't believe you let your employers have that much control over your personal life,' he huffed. 'I really can't understand why having a Facebook page would be such a bad thing.'

My employers spent a fortune on agents, managers and publicists to control their public image, and a virtual portal into their real life could do a lot of damage.

I knew a British nanny who was fired for posting a 'selfie' taken in her boss's kitchen. The mum was a celebrity chef and the face of a national supermarket. In the background of the photograph you could see a supermarket receipt stuck to the door of the fridge. The problem was that the weekly food shop hadn't been done at the supermarket the chef represented, but at their cheaper competitor. An eagle-eyed reporter zoomed in on the photograph and broke the story with the headline, 'The taste of hypocrisy.' Her boss lost a three million dollar endorsement deal, all because the nanny wanted to tweet a photo of her new haircut.

'Well, I don't understand all the fuss about Facebook,' I replied. 'It just seems like such a waste of time to me. If I have a moment to myself I'd rather sleep or phone you for a proper conversation. I want to hear your voice, not just look at a photo of you that was taken at the Easter show seven years ago. You need to update that, by the way. It's false advertising.'

I had once searched Will's name on Facebook just to see what his profile said about him. Because I couldn't log in to the site all I could read was his age, his job title and the fact his favourite film is *The Man from Snowy River*.

But that was just another reason I didn't want a Facebook account. 'What would I update anyway?' I asked Will. 'I wouldn't be able to write anything about my job or the children that I work for, and what topics would that leave me with?' My friends, hobbies and worries all revolved around my work, which is a sad realisation when you're meant to be in the prime of your life.

'It's not all about you, Lindsay,' he laughed, and then seemed to remember he was at work and lowered his voice. 'You can use it to keep track of your friends back home, like me. Tons of people are just Facebook watchers and don't write anything. They're just interested in other people.'

That didn't sound like much fun to me. I'd rather not read what people that I went to school with are doing. 'Rachel just got engaged. Hayley is having a baby.' I suspect that my old school friends back in Hamilton would envy my life in Los Angles, but the reality is I've been working full time since I finished school, and a constant stream of Facebook announcements of engagements, house purchases and newborns would give me pangs of envy for normality.

I feel like I grew up too fast sometimes. While my friends were sneaking in to nightclubs and kissing boys, I was doing night-feeds and singing nursery rhymes. I've been at the mercy of a boss and a handful of children since I was still a child myself, and sometimes I can't help feeling like I've missed out.

As a sixteen-year-old, I used to get embarrassed when I had to take the Stavros children to the shopping mall, in case I bumped into any of my old school friends. On the benches outside the cinema, there'd always be a group of girls from my high school, flirting with the popular boys. I'd be pushing a stroller with a wailing baby, juggling nappies and wiping kids' noses.

I certainly didn't look like a celebrity back then. I looked like a teen mum who needed a lesson on contraception. If I walked past a group of grandmothers, one was sure to make a derogatory comment. 'No ring on her finger. What is the world coming to?'

I've lost a lot of friends over the years because our lives have moved in such different directions. When my sixteen-year-old school friends had been excited by the launch of a new range of crimping irons, I was buying diapers and knew far too much about nappy rash cream.

I'm sure those popular girls would be envious of my glamorous life now, but I also felt a twinge of jealousy when I heard about theirs. I sometimes imagine what it would be like to own an apartment, where I could invite friends over for dinner.

I could have explained all this to Will but it sounded so depressing and insecure. 'It's fine,' I sighed. I overheard someone talking to him in the background—it sounded like the receptionist telling him his next meeting had arrived. 'Why don't you call me whenever you're free. I'll keep my mobile on me and if I don't answer straight away I'll call you back from a phone booth as soon as I can.' It seemed like a compromise and would hopefully appease Will, who was obviously growing impatient with my restrictions.

I haven't admitted this to anyone, but for the past year I've been having the same anxiety dream at least once a week. I'm standing in my old street in Hamilton, in the ball gown that I wore to last year's Oscars party. A huge diamond the size of a boulder is chained to my ankle, as if I'm a prisoner. I realise that I have no job and no money. I'm knocking on my old front door but my parents aren't home or don't want to answer.

8

'*Lindsaaay*, the chef has quit. You're going to have to cook until we find a replacement.'

As if my life wasn't busy enough, now I had to add chef to my repertoire. You'd think that Alysha would be able to find another cook in a heartbeat, but she's particularly picky when it comes to her kitchen hands. The last chef had been headhunted from a Michelin starred restaurant in New York City. Her last words, as she stormed out of the house, were 'I'd rather work at McDonald's than around this madness!' The reality television producers *loved* the drama and asked the chef if she could do a second take, but this time look even angrier. 'Maybe you could throw a punch at Alysha as you walk out the door?' asked the producer hopefully. The chef didn't agree, although it must have been tempting.

Her resignation was brought on by Alysha's latest weight-loss regime, which was called the 'air diet' and was more of a non-eating plan. The chef had to prepare Alysha's favourite meals, which she would then hold to her nose and sniff, but not eat. For the chef, this latest diet was the final nail in the coffin. She saw it as an insult to her culinary talents—and who could blame her? It reminded me of an actress I worked for who would buy all of her favourite foods—meat pies, doughnuts, tubs of frosting—and then stand at the kitchen sink, chew mouthfuls and spit them down the plughole. She claimed it was the secret to her sixteen-inch waist, as she could satisfy her tastebuds with none of the calories.

I wasn't overjoyed at the prospect of cooking for six children and a staff of twenty, but it's not unusual for a nanny to be asked to flex her culinary muscles.

A lot of wealthy mothers have never made a single meal for their children; even something as simple as chopping up an apple or mixing a bottle of formula. They'll insist they don't have the time or the skills, which might be the case, but when they'll happily take singing and acting classes, even 'American accent classes', while insisting they don't have time to take a short cookery course, it's clear that it's really a matter of priorities.

As with all Alysha's food fads I knew the air diet wouldn't last long, so I wasn't too worried about the dangers. My size-zero boss was just having a crisis of vanity, because she'd seen the first cut of her television pilot and thought she looked fat. 'We're going to have to reshoot it all,' she ordered the producer, who looked like he was going to have a heart attack, and then asked me if I could get the contact details for Sharon Osbourne's gastric band surgeon.

She'd also put a padlock on the fridge and kitchen cupboards, which only the chef had the key to. I tried to turn this into a game for the children so they wouldn't need therapy. 'We can pretend we're pirates,' I said. 'It's like a treasure hunt and this is our treasure chest!' I don't think I convinced them, as seven-year-old Goldie had given me a disbelieving look and asked, 'Did Mommy stand on the bathroom clock and get angry again?' In the end I figured out that by 'bathroom clock' she meant the scales.

One of the trickiest aspects of my job is dealing with bizarre Hollywood diets, especially when these rules and restrictions are forced upon the entire family. It can be a nightmare trying to keep up with the latest celebrity food fads, and it was a sour subject that often came up at our Sunday-night nanny gatherings.

Last week, at the burger bar, Rosie had begged for my advice on how to handle her boss's culinary commandments. Her A-list employer was slimming down for her latest rom-com and had put the entire household on a vegan diet, including her three- and eight-year-old daughters.

'It's bloody ridiculous,' vented Rosie, whose British accent gets posher when she's angry. 'I wouldn't care if she actually had a moral issue with slaughtering animals, but this is just another fad. Every week it's something different.' Prior to veganism her boss had been a devotee of the Paleo diet, during which time Rosie had been sent to South

America on a private jet to pick up a crate of beef jerky. The week before that she'd put the kids on a three-day fruit cleanse, but all the fruit had to be grown and picked within fifty kilometres of their house. When Rosie asked why, her boss answered, 'Because I watched a documentary on it,' but didn't elaborate any further.

It was no wonder Rosie was struggling to keep up with the ever-changing fitness fads. 'As soon as I get a grasp of one diet she moves on to the next,' she moaned. 'It's playing havoc with the kids' digestion, and the chef is having a major meltdown. I don't know what to do, Lindsay, help me!'

Whenever one of my nanny friends butts heads with a mother about dietary regimes the first question I ask them is whether the children are actually in danger or whether the mother's demands are simply inconvenient. If it's dangerous then it's their duty to speak up, even though this can be difficult when faced with a famous mother with strong opinions and who is not used to being challenged. On the other hand, if the children aren't actually at risk, the best option is often to stay silent and wait for the fad to pass, as frustrating as that is. 'You have to play the game,' I told Rosie. 'I know it's difficult when you disagree, but you just have to do what you're told and try not to overthink it. You are hired to be a surrogate parent, but no mother actually wants you to challenge her opinion. The parenting decisions are still up to them.'

This might sound overly submissive but I've learnt over the years that a nanny has two options when faced with a difficult employer. 'You either have to accept the situation or leave the situation,' I told Rosie. 'If your boss is really too much to handle then it could be time to move on, rather than try to change their ways. If not, you just have to suck it up!'

I did feel sorry for Rosie because I could appreciate what she was going through. Alysha's tastebuds are equally erratic. If a celebrity is photographed in a magazine carting a smoothie or a takeaway food container, she zeroes in on the logo and orders me to find out where they've been shopping so she can copy them. In her eyes, making an unfashionable food choice is the equivalent of carrying last season's 'it' bag.

She's not the only mother who feels this way, which is why packing a kid's lunchbox is such a minefield. If you send a child to school with 'last season's snack' it will be the talk of the school gates. I'd recently been in trouble for giving Lavender her favourite chocolate bliss balls when everyone knows that trendy kids tuck into 'raweo' cookies (a raw, vegan version of an Oreo).

The hardest part of my job is when a parent asks me to put their child on a diet—especially when the kid in question isn't even slightly overweight. Since I'd started working for Alysha and witnessed her warped relationship with food, I'd been dreading the day she'd give me that order. When she asked me to take over from the chef, she clearly saw it as an opportunity to target her oldest daughter. 'I think Harlow could do with losing a few pounds, don't you?' she said. 'I want her to set a good example for her little sisters.'

I should have said no, as Harlow is a perfectly healthy eight-year-old; however, Alysha didn't give me a chance to answer.

'I'm thinking of booking her in with my hypnotist to see if she can help,' she continued. 'In the meantime, can you cut out all fat from her diet? And sugar as well? And if that doesn't work then try gluten too. And can you find out how Suri Cruise stays so skinny when she's always eating so much candy?'

I dug my fingernails into the table. I've studied child nutrition and know all about the dangers of removing fat from their diet. This also seemed like an eating disorder waiting to happen. However, I've been in this situation before and knew that if I said no, Alysha would remove me from the equation and get someone else to do her bidding. There are far too many private doctors in Hollywood happy to prescribe weight loss pills to schoolgirls, just as there are plastic surgeons willing to give boob jobs to thirteen-year-olds.

I'd just have to come up with a way that I could trick Alysha into thinking I was following her orders, without putting Harlow's health at risk or leaving the little girl with a complex and major body image issues.

When I was quiet, Alysha must have sensed my reluctance, but wrongly assumed that I just didn't want the extra workload. 'Oh, don't worry, you won't have to cook for long,' she added. 'I've just found an amazing chef from Chicago. Everything on his menu is cooked using wood or has an ingredient with wood in the name. His signature dish is salmon with wood-fired apples. Doesn't that sound delicious? I'm having the kitchen redecorated next week with a $60,000 wood-fired oven from Brazil.'

She then pulled an inhaler from her pocket, took a drag and coughed. The smoke smelt of chocolate and almonds, as if Nutella had been vaporised. This was part of her 'breatharian' regime. The inhaler wasn't for a medical condition—it was an appetite suppressant that was meant to satisfy sugar cravings.

The sickly sweet smoke had the opposite effect on me. After Alysha dismissed me, I went straight to my bedroom, reached into my knicker drawer and pulled out the family-size block of Cadbury Dairy Milk I keep there for emergencies, along with a big bag of fairy floss. The diet could start tomorrow. Today, I felt like rebelling.

•

Maybe it was the sugar high keeping me awake, but that night I couldn't stop tossing and turning. Around 1 a.m. I gave up and decided to use the extra hours productively. I sat up in bed, pulled a notepad from my bedside table and wrote a list of ways I could follow Alysha's orders without emotionally or physically scarring Harlow.

I already made sure the girls ate healthily and limited their fatty foods, although that can be hard to manage. The problem is, just as their mothers are gifted clothing and jewellery, celebrity children are given a free run of sweet stores and fast food outlets. Lavender even had a milkshake named after her by a global fast food chain, because they wanted product placement in Sir Cameron's next movie.

There are certainly strategies that I've used in the past when a client has asked me to put their child on an extreme diet that I disagreed with. I make tiny changes like cutting their bread into thinner slices, diluting orange juice with water and swapping ham for turkey. At least this shows the parents that I'm trying to cut calories, but I'm not putting the child at risk. They might lose a little puppy fat but they won't end up with an unhealthy relationship with food for the rest of their lives.

There was no way that I was cutting an entire food group from Harlow's diet. Unfortunately her mother thinks dairy is the enemy and refuses to even keep butter in the fridge in case it 'infects' the lettuce leaves. I would need to convince Alysha that removing fat wasn't a healthy—or fashionable—option. I spent the next hour surfing the internet, searching websites such as Vogue and Trend Hunter, for articles that talked about fats being trendy. I found a perfect article called 'Fat is the New Black' about how supermodels like Miranda Kerr are adding it to their diet. I planned to print it out and leave it conveniently on the kitchen counter for Alysha to find. She would be praising the virtues of avocado and almond butter by the time she got to the end of the page.

It was only 3 a.m. by this time, but I was still wide awake and the night nanny would be on call for another ninety minutes. So I decided to head to the health food store and stock up on supplies. In Los Angeles, health food stores are open twenty-four hours a day, seven days a week, just in case someone has a chia-seed emergency.

It might sound odd, but the thought of food shopping in the middle of the night, when the store would be deserted, seemed like the ultimate luxury. I can't remember the last time I walked around a supermarket alone, without a baby in a trolley or a toddler hanging off my arm. Even when I'm not with the Appleby siblings my 'nanny alert' never really switches off. I can't walk past a child in a pushchair without worrying about whether they're in reaching distance of a choking hazard. If I hear a baby crying I want to swoop in and comfort them, even though they're not my own.

So I was quietly excited as I pulled in to the store's deserted car park. When I walked in the aisles were as quiet as a graveyard, apart from a plain-clothed security guard pretending to browse the nut section. After a decade surrounded by bodyguards I can spot them a mile off, usually from their slightly bored expressions. I said hello as I passed by, and the security guard looked suspicious. This could have been because I was wearing my pyjamas, which I hadn't really managed to disguise by throwing a Burberry trench coat over them.

I would never normally set foot out of the house looking so dishevelled, especially when visiting this shop, which is a bit of a celebrity hotspot. I've seen the who's-who of Hollywood in this health food store, from Pink to Justin Timberlake and the entire LA Galaxy football team. You never know who you might bump elbows with over the sweet potatoes, although I don't tend to get starstruck. In this business, it's not unusual to walk into the living room and find your idols sitting on the sofa watching themselves on TV.

So I'm not sure why I was so stunned to bump into Tommy Grant, the new golden boy of the golfing world. I'm not even a sports fan but I recognised him immediately. When not winning every trophy on the circuit, Tommy, and his supermodel girlfriend, Sophia Balmain, were being photographed at the hottest parties. He was also drop-dead gorgeous, with dark scruffy hair and a permanent five o'clock shadow. He always wore a pendant around his neck with the letter 'S'. His mum Sharon was his number one fan and never missed a tournament.

Tommy and his girlfriend were such a beautiful couple that I'd heard a rumour Armani had already signed up their future children to model for their junior range, although that could be an exaggeration.

Sophia was a stunning brunette who used to be a ballerina. Whenever I saw her on TV she seemed to glide with grace and poise. I, on the other hand, smashed straight into Tommy with my trolley, scattering a box of quinoa across the floor.

'I'm so, so sorry,' I apologised, feeling my face grow red, as he staggered backwards. He was carrying a shopping basket and I automatically scanned the contents. It had a bottle of ginger beer, a packet of vegetable chips and a portion of vegan cheesecake for one.

It took a moment for the sports star to get his breath back, but when he spoke his voice was deeper than I'd imagined. 'No need to apologise,' he puffed. 'It's nice to see I'm not the only lunatic shopping in the middle of the night. I started to feel like that guy in *I Am Legend*.'

He scanned my face, looking puzzled. 'Do I know you from somewhere?' he asked. 'I feel like we've met before. Am I being extremely rude by not recognising you?'

This left me in a bit of a tricky situation, as our paths had crossed before, but I wasn't really at liberty to tell him where. I had once worked for Tommy's predecessor—the previous golden boy of the golfing world, who had made some unfortunate choices in his private life that had seen him fall from grace. Tommy used to visit our house every now and again, although we hadn't ever spoken.

He and Sophia had also attended a charity ball at Alysha's mansion, although I'd only glimpsed them from across the room. However, I wasn't really supposed to broadcast who I worked for, even though Tommy wasn't exactly a reporter. I could have told him if I wanted to, but I found myself dodging the question.

'I think I just have one of those faces,' I stammered. 'Although I recognise you from . . . you know . . . everywhere.'

I kicked myself for sounding like such a pathetic groupie but, thankfully, Tommy laughed. 'Yep, I'm sure people are sick of looking at me,' he said. 'That's why I prefer shopping in the dead of night. Oh, and I'm horrifically jetlagged. I just flew in from London.'

Now *this* was a topic that I could talk about. I like to think that I'm a bit of an expert on long-haul travel. 'Oh, you should try an extract called Pycnogenol,' I said excitedly. 'It's a type of tree bark that helps you reset your body clock. It's my lifesaver! And when we're travelling I give my children garlic oil to stop their ears hurting on take-off.'

At this, Tommy raised his eyebrows. 'You look far too young to have children,' he said. 'But thanks for the tip. I'll have to try it next time I'm travelling.' Then, before I could correct his mistake, he looked towards the exit. 'Anyway, it was nice to meet you,' he said. 'I'd better get my slice of cheesecake home to bed.'

As he walked away down the aisle I kicked myself for not correcting him. Now he thought I had kids. He'd probably assume I was married. I'm not sure why this bothered me so much, or what came over me next. I blame lack of sleep or the free samples of maca powder that I'd eaten at the entrance to the shop—the label had warned that it's an aphrodisiac.

Instead of finishing my shopping, I dumped my trolley in the gluten-free section and followed Tommy around the supermarket like a stalker. I kept one aisle behind him so that he wouldn't notice, peering through the shelves of dried fruit and muesli between us.

I watched as Tommy added a tin of soup to his basket and then choose a baguette from the bakery section. I watched him deliberate for five minutes over two types of chemical-free shampoo and then buy neither. I found myself imagining what his kitchen would look like and what he'd smell like in the shower.

At the freezer section I gave myself a good hard talking-to. 'Lindsay Starwood, get it together. You are losing your marbles.' I didn't even realise I had said it out loud until Tommy turned around and stared at me.

'Hello again,' he said, sounding surprised. 'Are you okay? You look sort of lost.' I was suddenly very aware that

I didn't even have a shopping trolley anymore, as I'd left it behind four aisles ago.

'Umm, yes,' I stuttered. 'I just realised that I left my wallet at home. I better run back and get it. It was nice to meet you . . . again!'

Then I raced out of the store before he could do something chivalrous like offering to pay for my shopping. Once I was safely back in my car I breathed a sigh of relief, until I glanced in the rear-view mirror and saw what I looked like. Not only was I wearing pyjamas, but my fringe was clipped back with a pink, glittery Barbie comb that Lavender had stuck in my hair the previous night when we'd been playing hair salon.

Still, it could be worse. I'd once answered the front door to a delivery guy who I had a crush on wearing pull-up pants over my jeans, like I was Superman. I was toilet-training a little boy at the time and had been showing him how to put them on. The problem was I then forgot that I was wearing them. To make matters worse, they had a Mickey Mouse face printed on the crotch and Daffy Duck printed on the backside. (I'm amazed they fit me, but the little boy in question was the heir to a chocolate brand and a little . . . plus-sized.) I thought the delivery guy was checking out my bum as I walked away, until I looked in the mirror.

If I was Carrie Bradshaw maybe I could pull these looks off, but I don't think Tommy would believe it was an ironic fashion statement.

Maybe tomorrow I'd put in a call to my former boss, a New York fashion designer, and ask her to tweet a photo of a Barbie hairclip. That's all it took to start a fashion trend these days. Tommy's girlfriend would probably want one by the end of the week. Then again, why did I care what he thought anyway?

9

'Mommy, I don't want a bullion, I just want a bicycle!'

Lavender's fourth birthday was coming up, and she was unimpressed with the present her parents planned to give her. I was just amazed that a four-year-old had the word 'bullion' in her vocabulary. It's basically a brick of solid gold, which can weigh up to one kilogram. It was the current hottest trend in kids' birthday gifts. They have to be kept in the family's vault in the bank, which is why Lavender was disappointed. 'I want a present that I can *play* with,' she hollered.

The Appleby household was currently gearing up for Lavender's birthday party next weekend, as if juggling a film crew wasn't enough to keep us busy. Of course, Alysha wasn't organising it herself, as she rarely got her hands dirty. This is the woman who if her daughter wants a glass of water, calls me on my mobile to ask me to fetch it. She doesn't know the meaning of 'do-it-yourself'.

Instead she'd hired the best party planner in the city—Giovanni Joseph, the man who had imported live zebras for Elton John's black and white ball. I suspected that Lavender's fourth birthday party had the same over-the-top budget and vast expectations as his previous client had had.

It wasn't that Lavender was spoilt. The birthday girl, who was the most introverted of the sisters, would be more than happy with a more modest 'cake and balloons' celebration. However, Alysha was pulling out all the stops to make it perfect. In this town, children's birthday parties are a multi-million-dollar business.

When I'd suggested that we cut the party guests down from one hundred and fifty people to a more frugal number, my boss had given me a lecture on the financial expectations of hosting a junior Hollywood celebration. 'When you're planning the budget, you have to multiply the kid's age by $10,000.' That meant Lavender's party would have a price tag of at least $40,000.

The theme of the event was 'Barbie's Malibu Dreamhouse', which had been chosen by Alysha, not Lavender herself. An email had been sent to all of the casting agencies in America, asking for models or actresses who shared the famous doll's vital statistics. If she were a real woman Barbie would apparently have a 36-inch bust, 18-inch waist and 33-inch hips. In a city where plastic surgery is rife, it was shockingly easy to find models with these odd proportions. Fernando had put in a bulk order for a special type of shiny foundation, which he'd paint all over their skin to make them look plastic. When the young guests arrived at the front gates of the mansion they would be greeted by an army of life-size Barbies and Ken dolls.

A fleet of fifty miniature pink Cadillacs would be waiting at the entrance to the mansion, so the young party-goers could drive themselves to the back garden, where a marquee would be set up. Each car had a number plate personalised with the child's name, and they'd be given the Cadillac as a going-home gift.

The grass, the trees and even five toy poodles would be coloured a bubblegum pink to match the Barbie theme. There would also be a 'pink carpet', where the guests could pose for photographs, and a pink candy bar, where the kids could overdose on red liquorice, fairy floss, marshmallows, pink jelly babies and red velvet cupcakes.

I would never admit this to Alysha, but I thought the entire theme was kind of clichéd, especially compared to some of the children's parties that I'd attended in the past year. My favourite was the skater girl party, where an eight-year-old's parents built an elaborate skate park in their back garden and had a guest appearance from Tony Hawk, as well as a graffiti artist who customised a skateboard for every guest. Admittedly the atmosphere was dampened when one guest fell off the top ramp and broke her arm, but at least the idea was original.

I also loved the winter wonderland party that was held in the middle of summer. The mother was a singer who'd made a fortune from a Christmas number one, so was overly attached to the season. The huge lawn was covered with artificial snow; there were real penguins and even a seal in the swimming pool. There were also huge ice sculptures shaped like the eight-year-old birthday girl and her parents. Fernando and I joked that it was a perfect replica of the mother, whose face was frozen from Botox anyway.

A friend of Goldie's had a Willy Wonka birthday party. His dad owned a chocolate company and the gold invitations came wrapped inside a block of chocolate.

However, even these were just the tip of the iceberg, given the parties I've attended around the world. There were parents who flew sixty children first class from Hollywood to Disneyland . . . in Paris. And the London businessman who booked the whole of Harrods for his son's party. He gave every ten-year-old guest a five hundred pound gift card and organised a miniature steam train to drive them around the store.

It wasn't as though the Applebys hadn't been known to go all out, though. Last Easter we had an egg hunt in the garden and invited fifty of the littlest movers and shakers in Hollywood. I was given the task of hiding two thousand chocolate eggs in the garden. However, in addition to the candy, I also hid a hundred plastic balls with fifty dollar notes inside. I tried to counteract Alysha's desire to show off her wealth with a little bit of home-grown magic—I made Easter Bunny footprints on the floor with talcum powder and spent an entire afternoon picking brown jelly beans out of bags of Jelly Bellys so I could scatter them around like rabbit poo.

The stakes were even higher with Lavender's birthday, because the event was going to be filmed for Alysha's TV show. We'd had to send release forms with all of the party invitations, asking for permission to show their children's faces on film. I thought this might put some parents off attending, but it had the opposite effect. Usually it's the nanny who has to chaperone kids to a party, but the film crew was proving to be a drawcard.

I was helping the girls as they were having final measurements taken for their Barbie costumes when Rosie phoned me in a panic. 'Terrible news,' she hissed, 'my boss wants to come to the birthday party too. She's suddenly decided she wants to spend quality time with her daughters. I can't imagine why.' It was the same reason over seventy mothers had sent an RSVP—hoping that it would boost their profiles.

That's why I was dreading the party. It's a dangerous concoction, putting children who aren't used to sugar in a room with parents who aren't used to being around children.

'I'm sorry, Rosie,' I said, ducking in to the movie theatre, which was the only soundproof room in the mansion. 'I'm also so, so sorry about the dress code. It obviously wasn't my idea, and I tried to warn Alysha it could get complicated.'

Every child had been told to come dressed as a different Barbie. This seemed easy in theory, as she'd had a lot of personas over the years, from doctor to astronaut, lifeguard and flight attendant. The problem was that every mother wanted her daughter to come dressed as Pony Club Barbie so that she could ride into the party on a real horse and steal the show. There was currently a group email going around at least eight mothers, arguing about why their child should get the honour. Luckily, the birthday girl was going as Bridal Barbie, wearing a miniature wedding dress custom-made by Vera Wang.

'Oh, I forgot to tell you,' said Rosie before she hung up. 'A friend of my boss asked me about you the other day. Some good-looking guy who rides a motorbike. He didn't tell me his name but he's clearly a somebody because he acted as if I should know him.'

This is one lesson you learn very quickly in Hollywood. If someone doesn't offer their name it's best not to ask, as if they're even vaguely famous they'll be offended that you don't recognise them.

My mystery inquirer was probably one of my former employers, I figured. Rosie's boss owns a baseball team, and I've worked for lots of sportspeople over the years.

'He asked if you were single,' added Rosie. 'He was cute, whoever he was. Have you got a secret admirer I should know about?'

I raised one eyebrow. It certainly wasn't one of my ex-employers—they would never ask about my love life. 'I don't know,' I replied. 'Maybe he was getting me confused with someone else.'

'Why? Because you're so hideous?' laughed Rosie. 'You really are oblivious sometimes, Lindsay. I bet *all* your male friends secretly fancy you.'

I instantly thought of Will, but that didn't support

Rosie's theory—he just seemed increasingly frustrated by me at the moment. 'You're living in a fantasy world, Rosie,' I scoffed. 'But thanks for trying to make me feel better about my spinsterdom.' An admirer was no use to me if I didn't know his identity.

'He also told me to give you a message,' Rosie continued. 'He said he'd see you at Lavender's party and that he'd bring the vegan cheesecake.'

•

What did this mean? How did Tommy even find out who I was and where I worked? And why was he sending me cryptic messages?

I wondered whether Rosie might be right, Was he *flirting* with me? I needed a man's opinion, so after I hung up the phone I headed straight to Fernando's make-up trailer in the courtyard. I knew Alysha was in a meeting with the party planner, which meant that Fernando would have time to deconstruct my love life for me.

When I knocked on the metal door of the make-up trailer and let myself in, I found my closest confidant sitting in a director's chair, with a blow-up rubber ring underneath him as a cushion.

'What on earth are you sitting on?' I choked with laughter. 'Is that Harlow's life-preserver from her Lifeguard Barbie costume?'

Fernando wiggled his bum and then winced. 'Oh, don't look at me like that, missy. I had an intimate part of my anatomy bleached this morning and it's a little bit tender to sit on.'

I opened my mouth to ask more questions and then thought better of it. I didn't want to be traumatised by the details and, knowing Fernando, he'd be only too happy to show and tell the area in question. I have to admit that it was hard to take his advice about my love life seriously when he was poised upon his inflatable throne, which let out squeaks every time he readjusted, like a whoopee cushion. Regardless, Fernando was the closest thing to a life coach I had, and so I filled him in about Tommy, our Whole Foods meeting and Rosie's Chinese whisper.

'I don't know why it's freaked me out so much,' I moaned, slumping into the make-up chair opposite Fernando and tilting it back so I could stare at the poster of David Beckham he'd stuck to the ceiling of the trailer. 'I don't even know the guy. But just lately I've been thinking how nice it would be to actually have a boyfriend, even though I know it can't happen.'

When I chose this career path I had to make a conscious choice to put my love life on hold indefinitely. I've had crushes over the years, usually on members of my boss's entourage, from security men to pool guys. I've only ever flirted from a safe distance, though, and it's never led to anything substantial. Instead I rely on my guy friends like Will and Fernando to give my life some male attitude when I need it.

'What do you want me to tell you, sugar lips?' asked Fernando, taking a slug of aloe vera juice from a bottle.

'I may not be a nanny—thank god—but I spend enough time around you girls to know that dealing with loneliness is just part of your profession.'

I hated to admit that he was right. When you're a nanny, it's almost like being a single mother. There is no other adult willing to cover your duties so you can go out socialising for a night. I'm not complaining, I'm just explaining—it's a widely acknowledged downside of the job. It's a cliché, but the children I care for have to come first.

When I go for a job interview, the most common question I'm asked by prospective employers is 'Do you have a boyfriend?' Every smart nanny will answer no whether or not they're single, because it's what the parent wants to hear. They don't want you to be in a relationship, because they think you're more likely to get homesick. You need to be focused on their children, not crying into your pillow or on the phone to your boyfriend.

It may sound unbelievable, but my relationship status is actually written into most of my contracts. If you check my file with the Applebys there will be a line in there stating, 'The employee certifies that she is single at the start of her employment.' They don't have the power to stop you from falling in love once you accept the position, but most clients rely on the fact that it's extremely unlikely to happen. Where would we find the time? Anyway, it's not like I'm starved for affection. I get plenty of love from the children, and I have little time to feel lonely.

'You and Alysha should bond over your abstinence,' teased Fernando. 'How long has it been since Sir Cam was last home? Six or seven months? I swear he only pops back once a year when he wants to impregnate her.'

'Shhhhh!' I hissed, glancing around the trailer as if my boss might Apparate in the corner like Voldemort. He waved his hands in a 'Who cares?' gesture. I sometimes forget how uncensored and fearless Fernando can be.

'You know, Lindsay, sweetie—in all seriousness, you should think about online dating or something,' he continued, oblivious to my scowl as he began painting his toenails with Chanel iridescent blue varnish. 'I know none of you nannies have time for a full-blown relationship because you're a bunch of martyrs. But that doesn't mean you can't casually date, does it? What about your Aussie hunk, Will? A fly-in-fly-out boyfriend could be just what you need.'

At the mention of Will I felt my lunch glug in my stomach, although I wasn't sure why he had such an unsettling effect on me. I focused my ill-feelings at Fernando.

'And how exactly would I have even a part-time relationship?' I asked. 'It would be a logistical nightmare. I can't spend a night away from this house in case one of the children needs me.'

Fernando pulled a face. 'Okay, I hear ya,' he conceded. 'It's not like you could bring a guy back here. Can you imagine the TV cameras catching the guy of your dreams sneaking in or out? Not to mention the fact that at least one of the kids seems to crawl into your bed every night.' We both let the reality of this sink in. 'Sorry, my darling, I don't know what else to tell you. That is exactly why I'm a superstar beautician and not a superstar nanny. I'd choose a romp over a rug rat any day, although I do admire and slightly pity your willpower. My bed is an over-eighteens zone for good reason.'

We both spent a few wistful moments staring up at David Beckham's six-pack. Then there was a bang on the trailer door and a male voice hollered, 'We start shooting in five. Alysha says can you bring the tear spray.'

Fernando reached for a clipboard with a schedule attached to it and ran his finger along the grid. 'I better run, Linds. They're shooting a "reunion" between Alysha and her sister, which is absolutely hilarious seeing as she's an only child.'

As I said goodbye Fernando gave me a smacker of a kiss on the lips and slapped my bum. It was the most action I'd had in a year. 'I'm sorry I couldn't give you better answers, gorge,' he exclaimed. 'It just looks like you're set for spinsterhood—either that or a career change. It is your choice to be here, after all.'

●

As I got in to bed that evening I half closed my eyes and stared at the empty pillow beside mine, trying to imagine what it would be like to have a boyfriend there looking back at me.

I couldn't remember the last time my bed companion didn't a) demand a bedtime story, b) wet the bed, or c) bring a teddy bear to cramp my personal space even further. As a nanny, would I always be the big spoon, wrapped around a teaspoon? It seemed very likely.

I've never admitted this to anybody, but sometimes I feel physically sick from homesickness. I've actually vomited from feeling so disconnected and disorientated. It's usually far worse when I'm away travelling with a family, as I'm thrown off balance by the lack of sleep, strange diet and hot climates.

I can't remember the last time I cried—probably because I spend so much time mopping up crocodile tears—but I have to find a way to let my emotions out somehow.

My homesickness seems to be getting worse as I get older. I don't remember feeling as lonely when I was working for Steven Stavros, but that's probably because he treated me like family. With power-hungry people like Alysha, you always feel like you're an outsider, which can be hard at times. I've learnt little tricks, over the years, for dealing with homesickness. I gravitate towards anyone with an Australian accent, because listening to anyone say 'G'day, mate' instantly makes me feel better. I also don't put up any photographs of my family because it makes me maudlin.

It's ironic, because I never have a moment to myself, but I've felt a constant emptiness inside me for about a decade.

That's why the Tommy situation had left me so unnerved. How could I even contemplate a relationship, even if an opportunity did present itself, especially if the man in question was a celebrity? With my insane work hours, we would probably spend more time apart than we would do together. I have enough people to miss without adding a boyfriend to the equation.

As I pondered the impossibility of the situation, my bedroom door creaked open and a tiny silhouette stepped into the light. It was Lavender, dressed in white pyjamas and a pink tutu, trailing her comfort blanket, which was actually a three-hundred-dollar Versace bath towel. 'Lindeeee, I can't sleep,' she whispered. 'Will you tell me a story? My brain feels too busy.'

It was nearly midnight but we were both wide awake, so I followed her back into her bedroom. I shot an evil look at the reality television cameras stationed above Lavender's beds. I had tried to stop them installing cameras in the kids' rooms but the producers insisted they needed a '360 degree view' of the mansion.

We crawled under the covers together, and Lavender pressed her little warm feet against my legs, which instantly brought both of us comfort. The book she'd chosen was Robin Hood. It was the Disney Version where Robin is a fox and Little John is a bear, and was currently her favourite story.

As I flicked through the pages, Lavender stopped me at a picture of Prince John, with a scowl so wide that it dislodged his crown. She pointed at his face and asked. 'Lindsay, why is he so grumpy when he has all of the money?'

I decided to turn it into a teaching moment. 'He's unhappy because his friends have left him,' I explained. 'He's sad because he's lonely. You see, sweetheart, money can buy a lot of things, but it can't buy you love.'

Lavender stared at me for a moment and picked her nose while she considered my comment. 'But that's not true, Lindsay,' she said eventually, 'Mommy pays you to love us, doesn't she?'

Sometimes kids have an amazing ability to see the truth in a situation. They also teach you things about your world that you'd rather not notice.

10

I'll tell you a secret. I can be just a little bit clumsy. If there's an opportunity to trip, fall or make a fool of myself, I'll probably do it. Don't get me wrong, my clumsiness never puts the children I care for in harm's way, but it does sometimes mean they end up laughing at me when I trip over my own feet.

You can imagine the chaos when I worked for the owner of a fast food chain who insisted that I skate around the house, wearing trainers with wheels in the soles, like all of the waitresses did in his restaurants. I have no idea how I lasted six months with no broken bones, although there was a lot of broken crockery. I used to get motion sickness after an entire day of rolling around.

On another occasion I ripped my leggings while playing Lego with the five-year-old son of a New York fashion designer. I was clambering up off the floor when I heard the tell-tale sound of fabric tearing. The little boy later drew me a picture to cheer me up—a perfect representation of the accident, complete with the gaping hole across my bottom and my purple spotty undies showing. I had to convince him not to bring the picture to school the next day for show-and-tell.

That hasn't been my only clothing catastrophe. I once destroyed a five-year-old girl's entire designer wardrobe by putting her delicates in the tumble dryer and shrinking them. She was delighted, as she ended up with the best-dressed dolls and teddies in town. Luckily her mum didn't even notice; I just called her stylist and ordered a new capsule wardrobe—one of every item, in every designer, in every colour.

Most of these incidents happened at the beginning of my career and I like to think I've got better since then, or at least better at covering my tracks. I try not to beat myself up about these minor accidents. It's not like I ever put a child in danger and I'm always telling the children they should embrace being 'flawsome'.

However, getting stuck in a children's playhouse was a feat of clumsiness even by my standards. Especially as it happened at Lavender's birthday party, in front of a fleet of yummy mummies, a film crew, and my crush.

•

I should have known the day was doomed when Fernando shook me awake at 4 a.m. 'Code red,' he hissed in my ear, 'Alysha is already up and on the warpath. You better get up fast and do damage control.'

I sprang out of bed. I make it a rule that I'm always up and dressed before my boss and especially before the children. This is not usually hard with Alysha, who's a notorious late-riser, but I should have guessed that she'd be up early on party day. I kicked myself for not pulling an all-nighter. I'd been awake until 2 a.m. anyway, cutting bangs into the hair of fifty Barbies with a pair of nail scissors. Alysha had decided the night before that she wanted each guest to be given a Barbie that looked like Lavender to take home. Unfortunately my fringe-cutting skills got progressively worse as the night got later, so some of them looked more like badly stuffed scarecrows, with hair sticking out at strange angles like tufts of straw.

'What's her majesty on about now?' I asked Fernando, as I yanked my hair into a ponytail and tried to smooth the pillow creases out of my cheeks. My best friend raised his eyebrows. 'Let's just say the apology flowers have started arriving,' he said. 'We're at six bouquets so far and another florists' truck just pulled in to the driveway.'

I inwardly groaned, because I knew exactly what that meant. Sir Cameron, who'd sworn that he would be there for the party, wasn't coming. It was the same on every special occasion, whether it was a birthday, their wedding anniversary or even Christmas. Sir Cameron would promise that he'd make it, his assistant would forward his travel itinerary and then, at the very last minute, an emergency would occur on set. 'I just have to stay and deal with this. The fate of the movie depends on it. Just tell the children that my artistic integrity is at stake.'

It looked like Lavender's party would be missing one important guest, although it would probably come as no surprise to the birthday girl. The previous week she'd drawn a 'family portrait' at school, which included stick figures of her mummy, five sisters, her favourite teacher and me. 'Where's Daddy?' I asked her. She pointed off the edge of the table and said, 'He's over there somewhere where we can never see him.'

Sir Cameron's apology would be followed by a fleet of florists' trucks, bringing bouquet after bouquet of Alysha's favourite lilies. I wish that he would pick a more imaginative way to make amends because it was such a waste: Alysha ordered the housekeeper to throw the lilies straight into the compost bin. I had started to associate the smell of flowers with disappointment and fury.

'I've got to run,' exclaimed Fernando. 'Alysha's been crying all night. I'm going to need to use all the tricks in my make-up bag to cover those puffy eyes.'

This was good news for me, as it meant Alysha would be trapped in Fernando's chair and not under my feet. I had a busy morning ahead, with six children to bath, dress as Barbies and take for manicures, including baby Chanel.

'Oh, and wait until you see what Daddy has sent to Lavender as an apology,' added Fernando sarcastically. 'It's in the garden. You won't be able to miss it.' When

Sir Cameron missed Cherry's christening he'd sent a sing-a-gram as an apology. However, this wasn't just any sing-a-gram, it was the leading lady from *Les Mis*, who suddenly appeared at the church and burst into a rendition of 'Amazing Grace', then bowed and hopped back into a taxi. Sir Cameron didn't know the meaning of understated, and I hated the way he thought he could buy his way out of people's bad books.

I made my way into the playroom, which had a balcony overlooking the garden, so that I could see what Fernando was talking about. It wasn't yet 5 a.m., so it was still dark, but the entire lawn was awash with pink spotlights that had been especially installed for the party. Under their glare, a team of seven construction workers was busy building what appeared to be a small cottage next to the swimming pool, which would later be filled with pink fluffy bubbles.

I recognised the logo on the crates stacked next to the construction. It was a Golden Door Playhouse—the kind that Tom Cruise had apparently bought Suri for Christmas. I'd logged on to the company's website out of curiosity, so I knew even their most basic playhouse cost $24,000. You were meant to get planning permission before erecting one, as it was basically the size of a granny flat. It had five rooms, including a living room, a study and a 'media room' equipped with a PlayStation 4 and a Blu-ray player. It came with electricity, running water and air-conditioning, and the kitchen had candy dispensers and a slushie machine. There was also the option of a vanity room with a manicure station, and a 'trophy room' where the child could display all of her awards and sporting accolades. From the size of the construction, it appeared that Sir Cameron had told them not to spare any expense.

'What are you looking at, Lindsay?' The birthday girl had wandered up behind me, rubbing her eyes and looking adorable in a pair of Burberry checked pyjamas.

I forced myself to sound excited. 'Look at the wonderful present that Daddy has sent you, Lavender.' She peered through the slats of the balcony, took one look at the men hammering below us, then turned and ran out of the playroom. This is exactly what I suspected would happen.

I finally found Lavender in my bedroom, hiding under my doona. She seemed to think of my bedroom as her safe place. Whenever she was upset about something it's where I would find her. Often, if her mum was in a temper because she'd lost an audition or her favourite lipstick shade had been discontinued, I'd come in to my bedroom and hear a little sniff from underneath my bed or inside my wardrobe. I keep a packet of Hershey's Kisses in my room to coax Lavender out.

'What's wrong, sweetheart?' I asked, although I knew the answer already. From my experience, the children of the biggest show-offs on the planet are often the most shy, retiring and hesitant. The truth is, many actors and actresses are also socially awkward and naturally introverted, but they just rely on drugs and alcohol to give them false confidence.

Like many rich kids, Lavender really didn't enjoy being the centre of attention. She was scared of loud noises, flashing lights and fast-moving vehicles. This wasn't great for a child who spent a large portion of her life travelling between crowded events while being trailed by photographers.

That's why I have developed a set of secret hand signals that my charges can use to alert me if they feel uncomfortable in intimidating situations. I came up with the idea when I was working for a controversial politician whose son would have constant nightmares about being chased by paparazzi. Imagine being a six-year-old in a busy airport facing a wall of flashbulbs and burly men all screaming for your parent's attention.

That's why I also teach the gestures to the parents and the security team. The grown-ups are sceptical at first, but soon realise the benefits of being able to quickly and subtly communicate in a threatening situation. Young children are far more observant than adults and seem to have an in-built radar for danger.

It's also a great way to communicate if our plans are changing, without any outsiders hearing. The children know that if an adult tilts their head a certain way it means 'stay close, walk fast and don't play with your siblings'. There are also signals to indicate that we need to leave a venue by the back door and that we need to split up and exit separately. I wanted to remind Lavender that I'd be looking out for her today, even though the cameras were in her house and the crowds were here for her.

'Sweetie, you don't need to feel nervous about today,' I told Lavender. 'If you feel uncomfortable, then you know how to get my attention. You only have to stay as long as you're having fun. Any time you want we can go and find a quiet corner away from everybody.'

The little girl nodded, looking relieved, and did a forward roll out of my bed and onto the carpet. I love the way that children can recover so quickly. They don't feel the need to dwell on things or hold a grudge unnecessarily.

'Can I wear my flashing sneakers with my dress today?' she asked. If it was down to me I'd have let her, but Alysha had ordered silver Chanel sandals to match the Vera Wang wedding dress. I didn't think she'd be impressed if I let Lavender wear light-up sneakers instead. 'If you wear the sparkly sandals this afternoon, maybe you can change into your sneakers in the evening,' I told Lavender. 'Your feet might get too hot otherwise. It's going to be sunny today.'

I'm pleased to say that Lavender's Barbie costume, despite the fact that it was a bridal dress, was surprisingly age-appropriate. It looked more like a ballerina's outfit, with a long white veil and sleeves designed to look like butterfly wings. I was sure it would be covered in pink paint from the grass by the end of the day, but it didn't matter if it was ruined. Alysha hated her daughters wearing the same outfit on multiple occasions. In fact, the sisters had a separate walk-in wardrobe where I had to 'file' any outfit they'd worn more than twice. Once a dress went in there it rarely came out again.

For the time being, I dressed Lavender in a Juicy Couture tracksuit with 'Birthday Girl' printed across the back that Alysha had ordered especially. As we walked into the garden, with four hours until the guests arrived, the place was in chaos.

'I said the dogs should be dyed *rose* pink, not *salmon*!' the party planner hollered into his headset as he sprinted past me. Poor Giovanni seemed to be on the brink of a meltdown, although, in his line of work, maybe that was his normal state.

In the kitchen a refrigeration chamber was being built around the cake, so that the gold leaf and chocolate ganache wouldn't melt under the film crew's lighting. Meanwhile, two-year-old Koko had got hold of Fernando's fake-tan gun and was brandishing it at a security guard. I quickly rushed over and disarmed her before there was a ModelCo massacre.

At least all this chaos took my mind off the question that had been driving me crazy ever since Tommy Grant had asked if I was single. *What about his girlfriend?* I'd stalked him on Google and they'd been photographed together at a party the evening after our supermarket collision. 'A source close to the it-couple says there's a wedding on the cards.' I suspected Fernando would have the gossip, but I felt oddly shy about asking him. So I did what I could to push it to the back of my mind.

The invitations had said the party started at midday, but nobody arrives on time in this town. By the time one o'clock rolled around and the first guests started to arrive fashion-ably late, I was exhausted from juggling the demands of Alysha, the children and the party planner.

As my nannying friends arrived with their children we exchanged sympathetic glances, knowing we'd all had a rough morning. I felt especially sorry for Opal, whose seven-year-old had won the right to be Pony Club Barbie. It made sense, as her dad owned the largest racing club in the country. Poor Opal was currently trying to coax a terrified pony down the driveway while mini Cadillacs whizzed around it. The little girl riding the horse was having a temper tantrum too, because her cream Ralph Lauren breeches were 'getting hairy'.

These kids really do live in a different world and think parties like this are normal. For them, having a full-size Ferris wheel in the back garden is the equivalent of having a swing set. The cast of *The Lion King* performing 'Hakuna Matata' on the lawn is no different from a clown making a dog out of a balloon.

For a while I busied myself in the gift marquee, where every guest's nanny had been instructed to drop off Lavender's present. At events like this it's normal for the birthday girl or boy to send a gift list to their guests, just as a bride and groom would set up a registry before a wedding. Alysha had even hired a security guard just to watch this tent. It's not unheard of for thieves to target kid's parties in Hollywood, because they can find such expensive loot.

When I'd written up Lavender's gift list, Alysha had ordered me not to put anything under one hundred dollars on it. 'I'm just teaching the children not to undervalue themselves,' she huffed. 'If these people want to be friends with my girls they should be willing to pay for the privilege.'

Lavender's wish list, which had been emailed to everyone who had been invited, was not modest. It included spa vouchers, an Armani Junior clutch bag, a miniature Range

Rover with cream interior, and an Audrey Hepburn Barbie in a display case. She's also asked for a Juicy Couture iPad cover, a six months' supply of coconut water and singing lessons. It looked like one guest had gone for the Dior snowboard, from the shape of a parcel in the corner.

Sometimes guests still buy 'off the list' because they want to give something even more elaborate and impressive. For Goldie's sixth birthday someone gave her an original Andy Warhol painting, which now hung over her bed next to a picture of Dora the Explorer. One of her classmates was given a ticket for the Virgin space flight, even though he'd have to wait until he was eighteen to use it. I knew a birthday boy in Beverly Hills who was obsessed with the James Bond film *The Man with the Golden Gun*. For his ninth birthday he was given a real gold gun, in a display case, with ten golden bullets. It's not uncommon for kids to be given gifts like this that are totally inappropriate for their age, such as getting a Lamborghini when they're a decade off getting their driver's licence. A lot of the children in Harlow's class already owned investment properties.

A second marquee, set up next to the gift suite, contained a hundred and fifty party bags, ready and waiting for the guests to take home with them. When I was younger I remember being thrilled with a bouncy ball and a piece of squashed birthday cake but among rich kids the stakes are higher, and it's a competitive business. Lavender's guests were going home with a party bag containing a Chanel lip gloss, a mini Polaroid camera that printed out stickers, tickets to the premiere of the latest *Toy Story* movie, a leather iPhone case and a bottle of perfume the birthday girl had blended herself. The loot was packaged in a real leather handbag, custom-made by an LA designer and embossed with each guest's initials.

Unfortunately, I couldn't hide in the gifts suite forever. As more guests arrived, Lavender wasn't the only one who was nervous. I am not a natural networker—not with adults, anyway. Put me in a room full of children and I can chat about Star Wars Lego, the new La' Petite Mini Cupcake & Donut Maker and the latest flavour of Sippah Straws all day, but I have a limited tolerance for grown-up small talk. Usually at events I busy myself with the children so I have an excuse not to join in conversations. However, at children's parties there is an army of clowns, circus performers and countless other minstrels to entertain them. This means nannies are left standing around and have to be sociable.

Luckily, Hollywood types have a short attention span, so few conversations last longer than ten minutes. I chatted to a fashion designer, two singers, the founder of a dating website and the inventor of a new diet pill that sounded like a lawsuit waiting to happen.

And then I spotted a guest out of the corner of my eye who made my stomach flip—and not in a good way. It was Sir Royston Kingston, a 62-year-old hotelier who I'd once gone on a blind date with. I'd been tricked into it, by my old boss Steven Stavros, who insisted he knew the 'perfect' man for me. 'He's rich, charming, handsome . . .' He failed to mention my date was in the same age bracket as my grandpa.

It was the worst date ever, not only because of the age difference but because he was an arrogant bore and a total show-off. When I arrived at the restaurant where we were meeting, he'd booked out the entire place just for us. It might sound romantic, but I like to have the background noise created by other people during a date, to cover any awkward silences. It also felt ridiculous having twelve waiters on call for our table.

I didn't have anything to say, which didn't matter because Sir Royston never stopped talking. His favourite topics were how much money he earned and how many houses he owned. At one point he even got out his iPhone to show me photos of his Bel-Air apartment, which had been featured on 'The Real Estalker'—a blog that profiles extravagant properties.

After six courses of bragging, I fled home and skyped Steven, who couldn't stop laughing and said it was the best practical joke he'd ever played. I was just thankful that Sir Royston hadn't tried to kiss me, although he had given me an open invitation to stay in the penthouse of any of his hotels. I'd told him I'd check my availability, but had never got back to him. I certainly didn't want to bump into him now, because wealthy men like Sir Royston aren't used to being rejected.

My gut instinct was to hide, but first I scanned the garden to check that my six children were safe and entertained. Currently, Goldie was in the playhouse, where she seemed to be running a McDonald's drive-through out of the kitchen window, passing food from the buffet to children passing by in their Cadillacs. 'Do you want to supersize that?' she was hollering. Sir Royston would never find me in there, surely. He had told me on our date that he 'deplored' children (not the best pick-up line for a nanny), and was probably only at the party hoping to rub shoulders with Sir Cameron.

Unfortunately, as I discovered, the Playhouse was like a prop from *Alice in Wonderland*. All the rooms had high ceilings and adult-sized furniture, but to get inside you had to squeeze through a tiny front door, which was barely larger than a dog flap.

I had to crawl on my hands and knees, which would probably have been fine, except that I'd chosen to come to the party as the gender-stereotype-crushing 'Builder Barbie'. I had a tool belt around my waist filled with plastic saws, hammers and a crowbar. It was one of these tools that jammed me inside the doorframe, with the front half of my body in the playhouse and the back half still in the garden.

'You cannot be serious,' I muttered, as I felt myself jam. 'Lindsay, you've really gone and done it this time.' I'm not a fan of enclosed spaces at the best of times, and no matter how much I wiggled and jiggled I just couldn't budge.

'We've trapped a grown-up, we've trapped a grown-up!' The children had noticed and decided to torture me. One little boy, who was dressed as Prince Charming, began bouncing a helium balloon off my forehead repeatedly. Goldie came towards me brandishing a bowl of pink M&Ms, assessing my face for an opening to stick them in. Outside the playhouse, someone started slapping my backside. I really hoped this was a child's hand. I had visions of Sir Royston Kingston fulfilling a warped fantasy.

Then, to my immense relief, I realised there was a telephone mounted on the wall inside the playhouse. This place really did have all the comforts of home! I managed to grab the receiver and dialled Fernando's number.

'It's Lindsay!' I hissed. 'Listen, this is an emergency. I'm stuck inside the playhouse. Stop talking about spray tan for a second. I. Am. Stuck. Inside. The. Playhouse. You have to get me out of here before Alysha sees me.'

I hoped that any other parents who'd noticed how long I'd been in this position, would assume I was playing a game, or at least not recognise me from this angle. A few moments later I heard Fernando's voice outside. 'You were not kidding, Linds,' he was laughing. 'You have outdone yourself this time.'

I wasn't in the mood to be ridiculed right now. 'Just get me out of here,' I huffed. 'And try and do it discreetly. If you help me I'll give you my Karl Lagerfeld backpack. I know you've been eyeing it off.' That quickly got his attention.

Unfortunately Fernando's methods were neither discreet nor graceful. He straddled me from behind, put his hands around my waist and heaved. I heard a loud crack and then I flew backwards into the garden. Fernando hadn't exactly pulled me out of the doorframe; he'd pulled the doorframe out of the playhouse. I lay dazed on the grass, still wearing my bright yellow builder's hard hat, with pink M&Ms stuck in my hair and a wooden doorframe stuck around my waist like a hula hoop. Around me a curious crowd had gathered, including the television film crew and Sir Royston Kingston, who was probably now thankful our relationship had been fleeting.

I didn't think it could get any worse, until a flash of metallic red at the entrance to the garden caught my attention. It was Tommy Grant, carrying his motorbike helmet under one arm and a giant cake box under the other. I can't imagine that his girlfriend ever ended up in these types of situations.

At that point, Goldie, who was still stationed at the play-house window, pointed straight at Tommy and announced in a voice that carried across the garden, 'Look, Lindsay, there's the man from your screensaver!' Never leave your laptop in the hands of a seven-year-old who studies web design.

•

Thankfully Alysha pulled in a bunch of favours so that my faux pas was not mentioned in the press coverage of the party. Instead, the *Hollywood Times* wrote a glowing report on the celebrations, focusing on the fancy dress, the pink fireworks display and the legendary guitarist who had climbed onto the roof of the mansion to perform a rock and roll version of 'Barbie Girl' on his Yamaha guitar. According to the gossip column he'd earned $80,000 for the six-minute concert. That was like pocket money to Sir Cameron, whose last movie made $1.2 billion at the box office.

The rock star's performance was worth every penny in my eyes, as it took the guests' attention away from me. I hadn't been able to face Tommy after I manoeuvred myself out of the doorframe. Luckily I had an excuse to escape, as Lavender had eaten too much pink frosting and was making the 'I'm going to vomit' hand gesture. I knew exactly how she felt; I felt sick to my stomach too.

We retreated to Lavender's bedroom and spent the rest of the evening watching Disney DVDs under her doona. I have a feeling she may have been faking her sickness to avoid the celebrations, because the second we were alone she perked up instantly and started singing along to the musicals, but I didn't mind having an excuse to leave the party.

Through Lavender's bedroom window, I heard the crowds break into the first chorus of 'Happy Birthday'. I hoped that Alysha wouldn't blame me later for Lavender's absence, when the editors of the reality show realised they couldn't find a shot of her at the cake-cutting.

I could understood the 'oohs' and 'ahs' of the crowd, as the cake was certainly a show stopper, with six tiers in six different flavours (vanilla, coconut meringue, pistachio, bubblegum, peanut butter and jelly, all gluten-free of course). It didn't have candles because the pastry chef said it ruined the 'look', plus Alysha hadn't paid $13,000 for a cake just to have wax drip all over it.

As the applause died down, I heard Alysha launch into the speech that she'd been practising for weeks in front of the mirror. 'Thank you all for coming here today to celebrate the birthday of my special daughter. The apple of my eye, the sparkle in my life. It can be tough for her having two such successful parents . . .'

It was typical of Alysha to segue into her own achievements. I wondered how many of the grown-ups actually realised that Lavender was missing, or even knew what the birthday girl looked like. As I stared out of Lavender's bedroom window, a giant pink helium balloon floated by. As I watched, a gust of wind swept it against one of the large spotlights. With a loud bang it popped under the heat, scattering pink feathers onto the partygoers below us.

11

In the aftermath of Lavender's birthday party I went into hiding, avoiding my friends' calls and cancelling the kids' play dates so I didn't have to face the outside world. When seven days had passed and I was still incognito, Fernando staged an intervention and left a note stuck to my bedroom mirror.

'Lindsay-La-La. You are coming out with me tonight. No excuses! No other nannies! Be ready at seven o'clock on the dot. Love, your fairy godmother. PS It wasn't as bad as you think, really!'

I had been planning to skip our Sunday evening nanny gathering. I knew that my friends would be sympathetic but I just couldn't face Madge. My nannemy had texted me the morning after the party, all the way from Monaco, where Doctor Jaz and his family were on holiday.

'I just heard what happened,' she'd written. 'You must be mortified. I feel so, so sorry for you.' That was not the reaction I needed. I already felt sick to my stomach every time I thought about my playhouse confinement.

However, Fernando was the one person I couldn't refuse, mainly because I knew he'd drag me out kicking and screaming. Also, I knew I couldn't hide forever, and the thought of a one-on-one date with Fernando wasn't as intimidating as facing a group of people.

At seven o'clock on the dot Fernando knocked on my bedroom door. 'You look terrible,' he said. 'A week without fresh air does nothing for your complexion.'

I was thankful for the insult, as it was one step up from sympathy.

'Thanks a lot, Nando,' I replied, using the nickname he hates, because it reminds him of fried chicken. He punched my arm and I thought how lucky I was to have him. Also, he was right—I hadn't brushed my hair in a week and I'd seen Alysha glaring at my ugg boots as I shuffled into the kitchen that afternoon. I was surprised she hadn't already given me a written warning for letting down the aesthetics of the house.

Fernando, who never goes anywhere without an emergency make-up kit, quickly pulled out a pair of battery-operated straighteners and smoothed down my blonde haystack. He then slicked on some Juicy Tubes lip gloss and I tried to smile at my reflection. I still looked like a character from *Lost* who'd spent a year in the jungle.

'That'll have to do, Linds,' tutted Fernando. 'Sometimes you just have to accept that you're going through an ugly period. But remember that it won't last forever. When your mood improves, you'll soon be pretty again.'

He wasn't trying to 'tough love' me, this is just how Fernando talks. He grabbed my Louis Vuitton handbag and ushered me out the door.

He had booked a table at one of my favourite restaurants, Japanoise, where you cook your own dinner over fire pits in the middle of the table, using chopsticks. On my nights off I love going to places I wouldn't usually be able to take the children. There was no way I'd mix food, flames and five-year-olds ever again. A few months before, when we'd been holidaying in the Bahamas, I'd taken the children to a restaurant called Flaming Cheese, where they set fire to the haloumi they melt onto the hamburgers.

It was the first time that Alysha had ever joined us for dinner, and would probably be the last. It really wasn't Harlow's fault that her flaming burger was held too close to Alysha's Hermès scarf, or that the scarf's fabric was so flammable. Apparently since our visit they now kept miniature fire extinguishers next to each of the tables.

I relayed this story to Fernando on the way to the restaurant and, even though he'd heard it before, he pretended that he hadn't. I think he sensed that I needed a reason to laugh, and instantly I felt better.

When Fernando and I arrived at Japanoise the waiter showed us to a table set for three people. The restaurant was packed, probably because *The New York Times* had recently run an article about how Sunday is the new Friday night. This town really is full of sheep.

A familiar-looking woman from the neighbouring table leant over and gestured to the spare chair. 'Is anyone sitting there?' she asked. 'Is it okay if I borrow your extra seat? I'm waiting for Ellen and Portia.'

Even though my pet hate is strangers who name-drop, I gripped the back of the chair to give to her. But before she could take it, Fernando stuck out his hand. 'Sorry, someone is going to be sitting there,' he said. 'Oops, sorry, Linds. Did I not mention that my new boyfriend is going to join us?'

We both knew that he hadn't mentioned our dining companion on purpose. I probably wouldn't have come if I thought I'd be the third wheel, especially if I had to make small talk with someone I hadn't met before. However, now that we were here I didn't really mind. I was secretly glad that it seemed Fernando had dumped his previous boyfriend, the male model, who had unexpectedly got engaged to his 'girlfriend' just in time for the promotion of her next movie.

Also, just getting out of the house had put my worries into perspective. The other diners weren't pointing and whispering, 'That's the nanny who got stuck in the play-house.' Instead, they were pointing and whispering about the socialite in the corner who had just returned from rehab after crashing her car into a ditch. I don't know what it is about celebrities and car crashes, but it seems to happen every other week to these people. On my first week on the job with Alysha she'd crashed into another car while driving her $100,000 Bentley down Hollywood Boulevard. She'd been pulled over for speeding a dozen times, and Sir Cameron had called in a favour to make a drink driving incident disappear from her driving record. It's no wonder so many celebs rely on a chauffeur most of the time.

'So who is the new guy?' I asked Fernando, who proudly pulled out his iPad to show me a photo of the two of them pouting into the camera. I recognised his new lover immediately. Caesar Lopez was a gossip columnist who had become a star in his own right. His website, 'The Daily Juice', got over 250 million hits a month and was always the first to break every celebrity story.

I'd never actually met Caesar but we knew each other from the 'circuit'. We'd first spoken over Skype when I'd worked for a singer in Australia who was on the judging panel of a television talent show. The singer had been running late for an interview with Caesar, so I'd answered the call and made small talk until she was ready.

When he realised that I was the nanny, Caesar clearly smelt an opportunity for a story. He somehow tracked down my mobile number and, ever since then, periodically called me to try and uncover gossip. He somehow always knew exactly who I was working for and intimate details of their lives. I wondered how many housekeepers, cleaners and personal trainers he recruited as spies.

I spotted Caesar immediately as he entered the restaurant. He'd recently lost three stone after taking part in a reality television diet show, and was wearing white jeans and a crop top, which showed off his new six-pack.

On the way to our table he detoured past the troubled socialite in the corner. 'Hi, Jasmine, darling. It's so nice to have you back. You're looking stunning.'

She didn't seem to notice the twitch of his fingers or the tiny flash from the camera hidden in his palm. I bet the photo would be on his website by the time we ordered our starters, with an arrow pointing to the white powder under her nostrils.

'My gorgeous Lindsay,' Caesar cried when he reached our table, 'how is the gorgeous Alysha and that doting husband of hers?' I had to admire the guy—he was certainly good at his job and never missed an opportunity. I'd heard that he had an undercover reporter working on the switch-board of the Hollywood ambulance dispatch so that he'd be the first to hear if a star overdosed.

'Stop fishing, Caesar,' I laughed. 'You know my policy when it comes to talking about my bosses' private lives. It's a no-go area and that's not going to change.'

I sometimes wish that I didn't have a conscience, because I know nannies who have earnt enough to buy cars, yachts and even houses just from selling stories about their employers to reporters. They get away with it because they're referred to as a 'source' or an 'insider'. I know nannies who have leaked photographs and medical records, and even planted recording devices in their bosses' bedrooms.

I could have made a fortune during my career, especially when I worked for Steven Stavros. When he divorced his wife and started dating Jamie, one celebrity magazine was offering $100,000 for the first photograph of them posing together. At the time, he and Jamie were refusing to leave the house.

As the weeks went by, the price offered for the first photo kept rising until it hit $290,000. I could easily have obtained a photograph, as Steven's phone was always left around the house and his pin code was the number on his football shirt. However, I just couldn't do it, even though I despised Jamie. I sensed that it was a slippery slope and, if I crossed that line, I'd soon be taking photos of Steven's bottles of antidepressants. A nanny I know found a positive pregnancy test in her boss' bathroom bin, which a magazine bought for $20,000.

I can understand why many nannies are tempted, as magazines offer ridiculous money for a story, especially if it's to do with marriage or babies. If a nanny refuses an offer of cash, they try other incentives, such as free holidays or cars. Some of these reporters have friends in very high places and offer to make parking fines disappear.

If they're stuck for a real story, a lot of journalists do make up their stories. An 'insider' could be another journalist who heard a rumour from a friend of a friend of a friend, who once brushed past the star in a supermarket. However, I do follow The Daily Juice because Caesar's stories tend to be eerily accurate.

After the waiter had taken our order, the gossip columnist continued on his specialist subject. 'So, Lindsay, I hear that Sir Cameron has been taking extremely good care of a particular actress while away on location,' said Caesar. 'I also hear that you're thinking of quitting the nannying game for good. If you helped me with this story, I could make a very generous contribution to your retirement fund . . .'

I frowned at Fernando, who shrugged his shoulders. 'I didn't blab,' he said defensively. 'This is all news to me.' I knew he was telling the truth, as it wasn't a conversation I'd had with anyone.

'Are Alysha's crazy demands starting to wear you down?' Caesar asked. 'Is it her temper? Her vanity? Her inability to eat solids?' This dinner was going to be exhausting if Caesar spent the entire time squeezing me for information.

I was opening my mouth to tell Caesar to cool it when his mobile phone rang. (Unsurprisingly, his ringtone was the theme from *Fame*.) He held up one finger to silence me before answering, 'Speak to me!'

As the person on the other end explained their reason for calling, the reporter's eyes began to sparkle and his foot tapped under the table. The moment the conversation ended he pushed back his chair and planted a farewell kiss on Fernando's forehead. 'Sorry, kidlets, I've gotta go,' he said excitedly. 'Big, big story about to break. Lindsay, you'll be particularly interested in this one. Trust me, you should keep an eye on the website.'

As he skipped out of the restaurant, I wondered which celebrity was going to be dragged through the gutter this time. I wish I could say that I didn't care and that I'm above reading mindless gossip, but I'm just as nosey as the rest of the world.

Fernando and I spent the rest of the meal bent over his iPad, hitting refresh on The Daily Juice website. When the story broke halfway through our dessert I choked on my chocolate mousse, and Fernando sprayed his aperitif across the table. After my coughing fit we both sat in silence, struggling to take the news in. Caesar hadn't been exaggerating when he said this story was big . . .

•

On The Daily Juice homepage was a photograph of Madge, my nannemy, posing next to her boss Doctor Jaz at a recent function. The headline read, 'TV DOCTOR DIES OF VIAGRA OVERDOSE'. A big cartoon arrow pointed straight at Madge with the caption, 'SHOCKED NANNY FINDS THE BODY'.

'Doctor Jaz has been found dead in his home after a suspected Viagra overdose,' read the article. 'The 42-year-old divorcee is known to have a heart condition. However, a source close to the doctor claims he was taking the libido-boosting medication to impress his new girlfriend, 23-year-old actress Ruby Garland.

'The Daily Juice have obtained a copy of the 9-1-1 call made by nanny Madge Crosby, in which the 26-year-old Australian tells the operator, 'I think he's dead! He's naked and there's an empty bottle of Viagra next to him.

'Although currently being treated for shock, Madge will shortly film an exclusive interview from her hospital bed for The Daily Juice.'

I was heartbroken for the ten-year-old boy who had just lost his father and felt genuinely sorry for Madge. I can't imagine the shock of finding Sir Cameron in that position. However, my sympathy for my nannemy decreased when

I watched the interview that she gave The Daily Juice an hour later.

In the 20-minute video, she was reclining in her hospital bed. Her hair was freshly curled and her lipstick perfectly matched the pink of her hospital gown. She had called Fernando from her hospital bed to ask if he'd do her make-up for the interview, but he'd refused with typical Fernando frankness. 'I'm sorry, Madge, but I just can't do it,' he said. 'Firstly, I really don't like hospitals, and also I really don't like you. Soz, babes!'

After talking about the shock of finding Doctor Jaz's body she turned the conversation back to herself. 'I don't think I could possibly go back to nannying after such a trauma,' she sighed, dabbing a tissue to her cheek. 'I think the universe is sending me a message. Last week I opened a fortune cookie at a Chinese restaurant and the message said, "Build your own dreams, because if you don't, someone will hire you to build theirs." I think all this is a sign that I should follow my true career path . . . and become a singer.'

Then, to my amazement, she launched into the first verse of 'Baby One More Time' by Britney Spears. What she lacked in talent she made up for in volume. I couldn't believe it. She was pitching for a record deal while being interviewed about the death of a man who was a father and her friend. 'That girl is one smart cookie,' muttered Fernando.

He was right, in a sense. Within an hour that video had over five million hits on YouTube, and before the end of the week Madge had an agent and was moving to New York to record an album. At her leaving party I heard her boasting about the $50,000 compensation package she'd received from Doctor Jaz's estate. It must have been hush money, paid on the proviso that she didn't do any further interviews, as Fernando said Caesar was raging because she wouldn't return his calls.

'She has the morals of a snake,' I huffed to Fernando. 'I'm so happy to see the back of her. Good riddance!' However, I was surprised to feel an emotion that resembled envy. I hated to admit it, but a tiny part of my subconscious was jealous because Madge had found an escape route. It's not that I wanted to leave my job anytime soon, but I sometimes wondered how long I could keep up the long hours and the extreme demands.

I had, on previous occasions, had doubts about my job, but usually only when I've worked sixty days straight and barely have the strength to lift my own head, let alone massage anti-cellulite cream onto a seven-year-old. At moments like this I sometimes fantasise about pursuing a Plan B, but the problem is I don't really have one. There isn't really a standard retirement age for this profession. Every now and again a nanny drops off the scene, and absorbs back into the normal world like a former Men in Black agent. Most nannies leave to have children of their own or end up working in the service industries, although that comes with a significant pay cut. I'm only twenty-seven years old, but I'm classed as a veteran in this industry.

I voiced my doubts aloud for the first time a few days later. As I tidied away the kids' dinner plates, I was surprised when my mobile rang and I saw my parents' home number

PHILIPPA CHRISTIAN

flash up on the screen. Had something happened? Usually, my mum appreciates that our catch-ups need to happen on my schedule.

As anyone who lives in a different country from their family will appreciate, every time my phone rings I fear it will be the phone call that will turn my world on its head; an illness or a terrible accident that I wasn't there for because I was on a trampolining date with the Beckham boys or snorkelling with the children off Richard Branson's private island.

'Mum! Are you okay?' I couldn't hide my panic as I answered. I grabbed the kitchen countertop to steady myself, and heard the whirr of the ceiling camera repositioning itself above me. The cameramen who remotely control them have a sixth sense for drama.

'Oh yes, my darling, your dad and I are fine,' my mum answered, and I let out the breath that I'd been holding. 'But we're worried about you. We read about that doctor who died and how the nanny found him. Is she a friend of yours? Why didn't you call us?'

Now that I knew everyone back home was safe, I wished that I hadn't taken the call at all. There is something about my mum's voice that makes me feel instantly vulnerable. I suddenly wished I was at home, sitting on the couch, beneath one of the itchy blankets she crochets.

'I'm okay, Mama, really.' I lowered my voice. 'It's been a hard week, but you know me. I'm resilient.'

In another country, which felt like another world, my mum tutted. 'You seem to be having more bad weeks than good recently,' she said, and I tensed as her words hit a raw nerve.

It did seem that way to me too. Either Alysha's demands were getting more extreme or my tolerance was getting lower. The previous week, I'd very nearly spoken my mind when she had confiscated Goldie's bicycle because 'cycling gives you thick thighs'. I later discovered the reality television team had scripted the comment. I couldn't understand why Alysha was allowing herself to be treated like a puppet just because a producer claimed that controversy was the secret to drawing in viewers.

'I really can't talk about this right now,' I told my mum, conscious that the ceilings had ears and everything I said was recorded. 'I'll call you next Sunday at our usual time. Oh, and if you see Will, could you tell him to call me too? I don't know what's going on but I can't seem to get through to him.'

My mum cleared her throat. 'I actually do have some news for you, dear, but I'd much rather tell you in person. I was thinking, why don't you come home to Hamilton for a visit? It feels like so long since we saw you. Your dad and I miss you terribly.'

It had been over eighteen months since I'd seen my parents, which was a long time even for me. Usually whenever I accept a job with a new family, I try to fly back to Australia for a quick visit, because I don't know when I'll next get the opportunity.

'Maybe you're right, Mama.' I surprised myself with my answer, as I usually make it a rule never to book a holiday in the middle of a contract. 'After the craziness of the past few weeks I could probably do with a break. I'll talk to Alysha and see what I can organise.'

'Really? Oh, Lindsay, that's wonderful. I can't believe I might get to see you soon!' The excitement in my mother's voice made me feel instantly guilty that I hadn't visited sooner and that I hadn't suggested it myself.

'It might only be for a few days' I warned. 'But it would be better than nothing. You better stock up on Vegemite and Tim Tams because I'm having withdrawal symptoms over here. Oh, and can you organise a chauffeur to pick me up from the airport with my suitcases?'

There was a stunned silence, then my mum laughed awkwardly. I realised she didn't know if I was joking. What did she think I'd become?

12

'Of course you can have five days off in a row. Go and spend time with your family. You deserve it.'

It was worryingly easy to get Alysha to agree to give me time off for a whistlestop tour back to Australia. In my contract I'm allocated thirteen days off a year, but very few elite nannies take their vacation allowance. That's why I got a sinking feeling when Alysha agreed to my holiday request so quickly. I was right to be nervous, as the very next day my boss called in the favour.

'Lindsay, I was thinking that your trip could be the perfect opportunity for the kids and me to visit the house in the Bahamas,' explained my boss, after summoning me to her sun lounger next to the swimming pool. 'Then you could fly with us to the Bahamas. It's practically on your way to Australia, isn't it? You're so much better than me at keeping the kids occupied on the plane.'

She was right about one thing (if not the geography of Los Angeles, the Bahamas and Melbourne)—I am a pro when it comes to long-haul travel with preschoolers, but only because I've had so much practice.

My high-profile clients, whether they're politicians, royalty, businessmen or superstars, have one thing in common—they fly a lot and, therefore, so do I.

I know the layout of every major airport in the world off by heart, especially the first- and business-class lounges. I could manoeuvre check-ins and security gates with my eyes closed if I had to. I've had to replace three passports in three years, not because they have been lost or stolen but because I've run out of pages to stamp.

As any parent knows, a long-haul flight with a child is a military operation at the best of times, but it's ten times harder when that child is from a powerful family. If we're flying with an airline, extra security guards have to be brought in, and the pilot and crew have to sign confidentiality agreements vowing they won't leak anything to the press (no celeb wants a paper getting photos of them drooling onto an armrest).

When you go on holiday with rich and famous children, there are so many additional factors to think about. The sheer amount of luggage is overwhelming, as you have to pack for every eventuality, from beach days to red carpet events and outdoor photo shoots. It's not uncommon for Alysha to tip off the paparazzi to our location and, if a photographer does whizz past on a jet ski, she expects the children to be wearing perfectly colour-coordinated outfits. She has a rule that the kids must have two swimsuit changes per day. It's a good thing private jets don't have luggage restrictions like airlines.

I wasn't exactly thrilled at the prospect of taking a detour to the Bahamas, but I sensed that my trip home depended on my cooperation. So, the plan was set. I would fly to Nassau with Alysha and the children, stay one night, and then fly on to Melbourne. While they were away, a 'travel nanny' would take care of the needs of the kids. In the Bahamas, so many famous families visit for holidays that there are nanny agencies that provide part-time nannies to cover their short-term stays. The good news was that I didn't have to accompany them on the way back, as they were only staying for the weekend. That's fourteen hours of flight time with six children for a 48-hour holiday.

Alysha loves taking 'speed vacations' such as this, where the length of the flight can be longer than the amount of time they're at the destination. I sometimes wonder if it's the novelty factor of proving she's wealthy enough to do so. I once overheard Alysha's accountant complaining about her travel budget—apparently a five-hour flight that Alysha had taken to visit a hair stylist had cost $35,000 in fuel.

I used to work for a businessman in Sydney whose favourite weekend activity was taking his private jet on a 'day trip' to Antarctica. They wouldn't even land, just fly around looking at the icebergs and then fly home again.

Some private jets are more extravagant than others. When I travel with royalty or politicians, their private jets have conference rooms with long boardroom tables, video screens and conference-call capabilities. When I'm flying with just the children they'll often use this room to watch DVDs or call their school friends while they're 38,000 feet up in the air.

I know a family living in Dallas who own three private planes. I'm not talking about small aircrafts—these are the size of Boeing 747s. They've decorated the inside of each plane like a house, so that when they fly, the five children can function as normal. They each have their own separate bedroom on board, eat in a dining room and then move to the living room to watch television. The kids still have to do chores on the plane and sit in a classroom to finish their homework. It's not like being on an aircraft at all. It's also spotless, as a team of cleaners are constantly hoovering and dusting, even when they're in the air.

In comparison to this, the private jet the Applebys own is relatively modest. It can seat up to nine people, but 'only' has one cabin and a bathroom. However, the bathroom does have a shower to allow Alysha to 'refresh' before disembarking. She often also flies with a make-up artist so she's never caught arriving anything but #flawless.

The week before Alysha flies I have to send the head of the cabin crew a 'rider', which is basically a list of food and drinks she needs on board, plus any special requirements to make her journey enjoyable. I always feel deeply embarrassed sending this type of list to the charter company, as some of the demands can be so ridiculous. Alysha insists on only drinking 'diamond water', which is blessed by 'priest-esses' and filtered through real diamonds, according to the company that bottles it. On top of this, Sir Cameron Appleby insists the in-flight entertainment system only plays movies that he's directed—even if he's not actually flying.

'Tell the flight attendant not to wear that horrible perfume she had on last time,' Alysha had instructed. 'It gave me a headache.' I had to tell the airline that Alysha had allergies and requested that none of the crew wore any man-made fragrances.

It was embarrassing to be making such fussy requests, but still, this behaviour was nothing in comparison with the demands of some of my previous employers. I once accompanied a teenage prince on a first class flight from the Middle East to New York City. During the trip he was served a $1000 desert made of edible gold and truffle ice-cream, which was served in a bejewelled gold goblet.

When I worked for the rock star Bryant Dasilva he insisted that all the airline staff, including the pilot, wear T-shirts from his band's official merchandise range. He also travelled everywhere with his pet budgerigar, Ralph, which flew freely around the cabin. He demanded that every hotel room we stayed in had a copy of *The Power of One* on the bedside table. I also had to pack a pedestal fan wherever we went, as he claimed he couldn't sleep without it whirring in the corner.

On top of the crazy demands and extra security measures, one thing that made travelling with the Applebys difficult was all the tweeting, posing and Facebook posting.

Thanks to in-flight wi-fi, every moment is an opportunity for a selfie. Here's Alysha reclining on a flat bed, wearing her in-flight pyjamas while sipping a glass of chilled champagne. Wish you were here?

I was hoping that, seeing as Alysha now had a social media officer, this would become a lot easier. However, as it turned out, there wasn't enough room for Crystal to come on the jet because a cameraman was also accompanying us. As we drove to the airport, Alysha added the job to my list of in-flight responsibilities. 'You don't mind, do you, Lindsay? Make sure you tweet even when I'm asleep,' she ordered. 'I have fans in different time zones around the world, you know. I don't want to leave them waiting.'

There's nothing like being trapped in a small metal tin with six children, your boss and a reality television camera. I spent the six hours we were in the air trying to convince the girls they *really wanted* to watch Daddy's movie about the big boat for the eleventh time, while trying to stop the baby vomiting on the leather upholstery and attempting to think of witty tweets.

I wondered how Alysha, who had popped a sleeping pill as soon as we left the runway, would feel if I snapped a photo of her drooling on her Chanel travel cushion and shared it with the Twittersphere.

•

The moment the plane's wheels touched down on the runway I felt my stomach constrict. The truth is, I have mixed feelings about the Bahamas, especially Nassau, where the Applebys have a home in a high-tech gated community. It's seen as the most dangerous place to live in the country, which is why I can never understand why you'd choose to bring young children here.

I've spent a lot of time in the Bahamas, as many celebrities have homes in the tax haven. I've worked for oil barons, Oscar winners, sportsmen and country and western singers. When you lie by a pool in the Bahamas you see private jet after private jet flying overhead like buses.

I suspect the Applebys only chose Nassau because it's sixty miles from the island that Johhny Depp bought for $3.6 million after filming *Pirates of the Carribean* in the Bahamas. Whenever Alysha brags about their Bahamas property it's one of the first facts she tells people. It's not all posturing, though, as it is true we once popped over there for a Thanksgiving barbecue.

Since I'd started working for the Applebys we'd spent a few weeks at the holiday home, always without Sir Cameron, whose schedule seemed impenetrable. I'm normally very adaptable to new environments because I move so often, but I never seem to be able to relax here.

The local police give out leaflets warning residents about the risk of home invasions, armed robberies and bag snatchings. On our first trip, the children and I were given a crash course on what to do if our house was invaded. We were taught to run up to the attic, where there were secret cupboards in the walls that we could climb into and lock from the inside.

The high walls around the community were designed to withstand everything from cyclones to terrorist attacks. The Applebys' property comes with its own private beach, but the security measures are so extreme that the children aren't allowed to set foot on the sand without alerting the community's security team. Sometimes it seemed less hassle just to stay indoors. Besides, you didn't really need to go outside anyway; when you pressed a button on the wall of the living room, the four walls sank into the floor to reveal a panoramic view of the ocean. There was also a pool that ran through the middle of the house, with a waterfall and lily pads.

The cheapest properties in the gated community are $1.5 million according to their website, which does a good job of glossing over the dangers. 'Come and walk our pristine beaches, socialize with like-minded people and enjoy martinis made the *right* way,' it advertises. There is no mention of the fact the American government had rated the crime risk for travellers to Nassau as 'critical'.

There are upsides to staying here; the kids love driving around the community in a golf cart, stopping to collect bananas and fresh coconuts for their breakfast. In the evenings we eat out in a restaurant, which has an aquarium with a 'real' mermaid swimming in it. The actress's costume is designed so that you can't see her breathing apparatus, which the children find mesmerising. I'm also addicted to the coconut chocolate they sell in the local supermarket.

However, to me it all feels like an optical illusion, and I can never quite shake a feeling of fear that ruins the paradise for me.

In my drafts folder I have an email that I wrote to Will the last time I was staying in Nassau. 'It's 5.30 a.m. here and I can't sleep. I've heard three gunshots and I'm scared because home invasions happen so regularly. My bedroom is the only one on the ground floor, so I've been sleeping under the bed. I wish you were here with me.' I never did press 'send', because I didn't want him to think I was a coward.

That's why I was thankful I was only staying one night in the Bahamas before flying to Melbourne. Nevertheless, it turned out to an extremely eventful twenty-four hours.

•

When I woke up to flashing lights, sirens and the buzz of helicopters my first thought was for the children. Whenever we're in Nassau I sleep in my clothes, just in case the worst does happen and I have to move quickly. As I jumped out of bed and sprinted up the stairs, the baby started crying and Harlow yelled out '*Lindsaaaay.*'

One of our neighbours in Nassau, the owner of an alcohol brand, has an imposing glass mansion that backs onto the ocean. From what I'd observed during our previous visits, he didn't speak to anyone and spent all day sitting on his balcony throwing fish food into the water. The lights and the commotion seemed to be coming from his property, although I couldn't be certain.

I found all the sisters awake in their separate bedrooms and, following the drill, ushered them up to the attic. I didn't make them climb into the cupboards just yet. They were already terrified enough as it was without being shoved into a confined space.

It wasn't my instinct to check on Alysha, and she didn't follow us up to the attic. She can sleep through a hurricane when she has her earplugs in and when I tried to call her mobile it went straight to voicemail. 'I'm sorry but Alysha is busy right now being fabulous,' trilled her recording. 'Please leave a message and I'll get back to you if you're important.'

The next call I made was to the reception desk of the gated community. A woman answered, sounding frazzled. 'Hello? Oh yes, we're very aware of the incident occurring. There's no need to worry. The police are dealing with it and residents are being advised to stay in their properties until further notice.'

That night was one of the longest of my life. The attic had no windows so I couldn't see what was happening outside but I was grateful when, within an hour, the buzz of the helicopters stopped circling and the sounds of angry voices outside died down.

I was glad that on my first visit to the holiday house I had stored seven sleeping bags in the attic for eventualities such as this, although I ended up zipping two sleeping bags together to make a big, cushioned sack that we all shared.

The next morning Alysha looked shocked when a policeman knocked on our door to explain the previous night's commotion. 'What noise?' she asked. 'Lindsay, did you hear anything?'

A bomb had been found under the alcohol tycoon's car, which was thankfully defused before it exploded. I was desperate to hear the full story and expected it to be the talk of the gated community the next morning. If we were in Los Angeles, the gossip columnists would have found the culprit before the police did. But the next day, nobody at the members' club even mentioned it. Is a tax break really worth your kid's safety?

As I queued at the local cafe to collect Alysha's morning espresso, the woman in front of me turned to her friend and gasped, 'I'm totally stunned. I just can't believe it happened.'

At last, I had found somebody who was as shocked as I was. Then I heard the rest of her sentence. 'I can't believe she was wearing a tracksuit to a restaurant. Does she have no self-respect?' I should have known that, among the Nassau mothers, a crime against fashion tops a bomb threat.

I was suddenly very glad that I was heading back to Hamilton, even if it was only for a couple of days. I'd forgotten what a 'normal' life looked like. I was looking forward to being reminded of what life was like without all the drama.

13

'I thought I told you to bring work boots?' My dad glanced down at my feet, which were encased in gold Jeremy Scott for Adidas trainers with angel wings sticking out from the ankles. I'd been given them by a former boss who was a major-league basketball player.

'But these are my work boots!' I told him. 'I've spent ten hours standing outside the Grammy awards in these without getting any blisters.' My dad, who was wearing gumboots caked in orange clay, shook his head, but his eyes were twinkling. Then he held out his arms for a hug. 'It's so wonderful to have you here, Lindsay,' he said. 'Your mother and I have been worried about you.'

This was a statement that I'd heard a dozen times since I'd arrived the day before. It seemed that everybody, from my parents to the milkman, the postman, the bus driver and the owner of the local corner shop, was 'worried' about me. I wasn't sure what I'd done to earn the entire town's concern, but it was starting to make me feel uncomfortable.

On the day I arrived, as I dragged my suitcase up the mud track to my parents' house, I was met by a slobbering pack of cattle dogs who leapt up and left dirty footprints down my white jeans. 'Hi, Rowdy! Hi, Rusty! Hi, Bandit!' I greeted my childhood family pets, who were growing grey around the temples. These were real dogs, not the little handbag rats you see carried around Hollywood wearing pearl necklaces as collars, with their claws painted pink. I was definitely home.

I had felt myself relax as soon as I buckled my seatbelt on the plane. I always fly home with Qantas airlines, because just hearing an Australian accent saying 'Welcome aboard' makes me instantly feel like I can let my guard down. I'd flown into Melbourne Airport and then caught a bus for the last stretch to Hamilton, pulling in to the bus station at 6 a.m. as the sun rose.

It was a strange contradiction, going from a first-class cabin where I was served caviar and smoked salmon to a rusting, rattling bus where I was given one biscuit in a plastic wrapper as the 'continental breakfast'.

On the winding walk back to my parents' house I stopped at a cafe and asked for a soya milk latte to go. 'I'm sorry, love, we only have full cream milk here,' the waitress told me, and I instantly felt like a diva for asking. I also instantly felt like a tourist, which was sad, seeing as I was born at the hospital just down the road.

It had taken me forever to pack for this trip because I didn't want to look like an out-of-towner. When I travel with my bosses I usually have to dress to impress, but when I'm visiting my parents I have the opposite strategy. Last time I'd visited my mother I'd arrived in a turquoise Juicy Couture tracksuit.

'You look like that girl from *Legally Blonde*,' laughed my mum, which I don't think she meant as a compliment.

I didn't want to appear flashy and I didn't want to look like a try-hard, so I left behind all my expensive accessories, as if I was visiting a crime zone rather than a country town in Australia. I also disregarded anything in my wardrobe that was covered in sparkles, had a designer label or cost over two hundred dollars. I was surprised to find this left me with very little. It was a good thing I was only visiting for three days.

My parents' house is on the edge of Hamilton, right next to a patch of woodland where I spent my childhood building forts and tumbling my bike into ditches. When I was little, there was only one dusty highway leading into town, and my girlfriends and I would spend entire afternoons just walking up and down it, waving at truck drivers to see how many we could get to toot their horns.

For old times' sake, I'd tried it on the walk home from the bus station, but the truck drivers had just nodded at me politely. It didn't seem to have the same impact when you were a fully grown woman wheeling a Gucci suitcase, instead of one of a group of giggling schoolgirls.

I love the fact that my parents still live in the house that I grew up in. There's something about sleeping in my old bed that soothes and settles me, even though my feet hang off the end. My old Singer sewing machine is still on a table in the corner. When I was thirteen my friends and I all had them, and used to spend our weekends making headbands and canvas bags from fabric we tie-dyed in my mum's washing basin. I wish I'd kept some of my creations, because Alysha had recently ordered a bag from a new up-and-coming designer that looked exactly the same as one I'd made, but cost $6000.

My parents' house no longer has a big plot of land, because they sold off their fields when I was a teenager. At the time I remember having a huge temper tantrum because it meant they pulled down my tree house, which was my happy place when I was younger. Now I suspect they sold the land to pay for our move to Melbourne, and I feel terrible for giving them such a hard time.

My dad still gets his 'nature fix' by helping out at a friend's farm down the road. On my first morning back in Hamilton he invited me to go with him to help repair some fencing. When I was little this was one of my favourite jobs, as I felt like I was assisting a surgeon when I passed him equipment from his tool kit.

It was a blast from the past visiting the Daleys' farm. I used to spend most of my weekends there when I was younger, as I was good friends with their daughter Britney. She was one of six girls and we'd all help to milk the cows and drive around herding the sheep on quad bikes. Talking to her parents, I discovered Britney now lives in Sydney, works for a global advertising company, and lives in an apartment overlooking the Harbour Bridge.

'You must be very proud of her,' I said to her mother, as I sipped a chipped mug of strong tea in her kitchen. 'She's doing so well for herself. Living in Sydney must be really exciting.'

When we were younger, Britney's mum was always the parent who led the standing ovation at our school plays and led the Mexican wave at our netball matches, so I thought she'd relish the opportunity to talk about her daughter's achievements. But instead Jenny seemed to want to downplay them.

'Well, Britney's certainly very busy,' she said. 'To be honest, her dad and I wonder how long she'll be able to last. She sends us emails in the middle of the night and she's always working on weekends. It's very impressive on her résumé but it seems very stressful. We do worry about her a lot. I'm sure your mum would relate . . .'

There it was again. That W-word. I wondered if my mother spoke about my career in the same way. I like to think she'd be proud of what I do—even boastful—but maybe she talked about me with pity, as Britney's mum did about her.

'You know who is doing very well for herself?' continued Jenny. 'Heidi McPherson, who was in the class below you at school. Do you remember her? She always had her head buried in a novel while you girls were climbing trees and rollerskating. She's the manager of the local bookstore now. I always see her cycling to work . . .'

I did remember Heidi, although we'd never been close friends. She was a pleasant-enough girl with perfectly straight copper hair, whose parents had owned a farm just outside of town. I'd bumped into her in the corner shop during my last trip home, when I'd been buying a copy of *Famous* magazine and she'd been buying the local newspaper. She'd asked how Los Angeles was treating me and whether I planned to stay there indefinitely. I remember thinking that it was odd she was so interested, but put it down to a small-town mentality.

'It's funny how some girls just land on their feet,' Jenny continued. 'Heidi's parents are so lucky having her close by. I met her mum in the supermarket the other day and she's so excited about the wedding. That Will is a lovely lad. You're close friends with him, aren't you? Did you help him pick out the ring?'

It took a moment for her words to sink in. Did she mean my Will?

Getting *married*?

I was embarrassed to admit I didn't know anything about it, so I nodded along as Jenny talked about how nice a spring wedding would be and how Heidi was wearing her mother's old wedding dress. I stayed long enough not to appear rude, while blood pumped in my ears, and then I thanked her for the tea and got out of there.

'Dad, I've got to *go*!' I yelled across the field to my father, who was up to his elbows in mud. 'I'll meet you at home. There's someone I've got to see *right now*!'

Then I ran at full pelt, taking a shortcut through the forest. It was a route that I'd taken countless times during my childhood. I raced past the rope swing where I'd got my first broken bone as a teenager, and the tree house where I'd had my first kiss with Will. We'd had our second kiss in the exact same spot, a decade later, when I was twenty-three. I'd flown to New York for a job a day later, and we'd never really discussed it.

As I ran my gold trainers slid on the mossy ground, and I cursed them for being all style and no substance. By the time I rounded the corner to Will's house I was dripping in sweat, puffing and panting. His car was in the driveway, and Will was unpacking boxes from the back seat when he looked up and spotted me. He had the same expression on his face as he did the day his mum caught us pouring dish-washing liquid into the duck pond.

•

'Will, why didn't you tell me that you're *getting married*?' I didn't waste any time. 'Is this why you've been ignoring me?'

I noticed that the boxes on the ground were full of fake flowers, fairy lights and rolls of white and gold fabric. A smaller box that Will was clutching to his chest was labelled 'wedding invitations'. As I stared, wondering if one had my name on it, he suddenly seemed to realise what he had in his hands and threw the box into the back seat of his car, like he was hiding the evidence.

'Lindsay, I wondered if I'd see you,' he said, in a tone that suggested he'd hoped he wouldn't. 'When did you arrive? When are you leaving?' I'd sent him an email when I booked my tickets, telling him my travel plans, although perhaps he was sending any correspondence from me straight to the spam folder. He hadn't really changed since we met on our first day at school twenty years before. He had the same inquisitive blue eyes, flushed cheeks and butterscotch hair that curled around the base of his neck. He was just a taller—and more muscular—version of the schoolboy I had my first crush on.

'I'm only here for a few days,' I said. 'Seriously, Will, it's time to drop the act. Can we talk?'

I realised that I'd have to take the lead, so I walked past him into the house and motioned to him to follow me. Will's parents had lived in this house until they had died. They both had heart attacks, four weeks apart. In the five years since then, decorating the house had become Will's pet project. For a while he emailed me a photo every week, of a bookshelf that he'd varnished or a tree trunk that he'd carved into a coffee table. I noticed the bookshelf now had twice as many books, and there was a handbag hanging on the coat rack. I didn't want to sit down, as I needed height to give me confidence, so I hovered in the kitchen, where there was an invitation for an engagement party stuck to the fridge. They'd held the celebration the night before I came home.

'Is Heidi living here?' I asked, looking around for clues. I couldn't bring myself to say the word fiancée out loud.

'Not yet,' Will replied. 'Her parents are very traditional. They don't want us to live together until after we're married.' He had recovered from the shock of my unexpected arrival, and was looking more comfortable. 'I'm sorry, Lindsay,' he said. 'I probably should have called you. I assumed your mum would have told you ... and to be honest I didn't know if you'd care.'

'How can you possibly say that?' I asked. 'Why wouldn't I care about such a huge development in your life? We've been friends forever. You know me better than anyone!'

His eyes flashed. 'Are you kidding me, Lindsay?' he cried. 'I don't know you. I *used* to know you. But I have absolutely no idea who *this* girl is. You've become a fully paid-up member of the superficials. Every time we talk you're on some crazy new diet, and every time we meet you've lost more weight and become more ... glossy.'

He picked up a lock of my hair and then let it fall onto my shoulders. 'Tell me, Lindsay, is it difficult to come home and visit the *common* people?'

I couldn't believe that my best friend was attacking me. 'What are you talking about, Will? Just because I look a certain way and dress a certain way, it doesn't mean I've changed. It doesn't mean that I'm a bad *person*, or that I love my family any less.'

As the words left my mouth, I thought about Alysha and all of the mothers who I judged so quickly without really knowing them. Was I really any different, or any better? In Will's eyes I was clearly just another superficial socialite with no grasp on reality. He walked to the front door and opened it, kicking my trainers that I'd left on the doormat into the driveway.

'Gold shoes for a gold-digger,' he muttered, and I felt like I'd been punched. 'Just go back to Los Angeles, Lindsay.

Go back to your friends and your celebrities and your parties. Isn't that your life's purpose? You clearly thought that was more important than staying here with me.'

He sounded like one of the children I cared for, who needed to learn that you couldn't be in their sight every second. I suddenly didn't have the energy to argue anymore. 'If that's really how you feel, then I'll go. And don't say my wedding invitation's in the post, because we both know that's a lie, and we both know I wouldn't come anyway.'

I pushed past Will into the fresh air, not even stopping to put my shoes on.

My parents were both sitting in the living room waiting for me when I got home, but I told them I was jetlagged and going to bed early. My dad raised an eyebrow, and my mum looked up from her newspaper and asked, 'I'm guessing that you went to see Will?' I nodded but didn't offer any explanation, and she didn't press me for details.

All I wanted to do was get into bed and torture myself by replaying the conversation in my head, like a child pressing on a bruise to see if it still hurts. Yep, it still hurt. In fact, it hurt even more every time I thought about it.

I'm not proud to say that I spent the next two days moping, lying on the couch in my pyjamas watching romantic comedies. Unfortunately, it wasn't as relaxing as I had hoped, as it's much harder to lose yourself in a movie when you've worked for most of the main characters.

14

Apart from the lack of time I have to update it, there is another reason that I'm not on Facebook—I don't need it. I can keep up to date with the lives of the people I've worked for and am friends with by heading to a newsstand and opening a gossip magazine. That is how I happened to read about the Applebys' divorce in the latest issue of *OK!* magazine, which I had picked up at Los Angeles airport while I waited for my luggage.

EXCLUSIVE!

DIRECTOR'S DIRTY DIVORCE:
HEARTBREAK FOR ALYSHA APPLEBY

It was confirmed today that director Sir Cameron Appleby has filed for divorce from his wife, actress and reality television star Alysha Appleby.

Sources close to the father of six, who, for the past twelve months, has been filming an action movie in Morocco, claim he has grown increasingly close to the film's leading lady, Cindy Berry, while on location.

'He spends a lot of time in her trailer,' says an insider. 'They certainly seem to be on the same artistic wavelength.'

There could be a reason that Sir Cameron has chosen to make the split public now. Cindy, 26, who began her career as a model, showed off a suspiciously rounded stomach when photographed relaxing on set last week.

'She keeps sending her assistant out to buy ginger beer and ginger biscuits,' says a source. 'The costume department have been complaining she's struggling to fit into her clothes'.

With a fortune estimated at $1.2 billion, this could be the juiciest divorce since Tom and Katie.

'We ask that you respect the family's privacy at this time,' said a spokesperson for Sir Cameron. 'My clients' priority is the happiness of their daughters.'

Now I understood why I had thirty-two missed calls and eighteen text messages when I got off the flight from Melbourne and turned my phone back on. My first thought was Will—was he calling to apologise? However, when I checked the caller ID, my frequent callers were Alysha, Fernando and several numbers that I recognised as 'friendly' reporters checking in to see how the family was coping.

The story had only broken that morning and *OK!* had the exclusive, with confirmation from Sir Cameron. I can't say I was surprised the Applebys' marriage was over, although I was surprised it had happened so quickly. I've worked for a few famous couples who've had high-profile divorces. They usually maintain the facade of a happy marriage for about a year while they quietly divide up their assets, find new homes and negotiate the terms before they confirm the break-up to the public.

It was also no longer fashionable to use the D-word. Celebrities don't divorce—they decide to 'uncouple and co-parent'. You can blame Gwyneth and Chris for this trend. I personally think it's better to call a spade a spade.

It was extremely bad luck that the story had broken the one weekend I was out of the country. It made me suspect the announcement was made by Sir Cameron without the knowledge of his wife.

I was immediately worried about the children. I wondered if Alysha had had a chance to tell them before the rest of the world found out. Unfortunately, the kids of celebrities are often the last to know about the milestones in their parents' lives. Somewhere between informing their agents, lawyers, publicity team and favourite talk-show host, they seem to run out of time to tell the news to their own flesh and blood. One of my previous bosses had proposed to his new girlfriend and sold their engagement photo to a magazine without first telling his teenage children. His divorce from their mother had only been announced two weeks earlier, and they'd only met the new girlfriend once.

Then suddenly their daddy and 'new step-mommy' were on the front cover of a magazine gushing about the 'new chapter in our lives'.

As my taxi pulled up outside the Appleby mansion there was much excitement among the gathered crowd of paparazzi, who thought I was Alysha. I'd recently been told the word paparazzi means 'buzzing mosquito' in Italian. I tried to google it and decided it must be an urban myth, but I still think it's a brilliant translation. That's exactly what they remind me of—hundreds of overexcited little men, running around in circles, trying to suck your blood.

Even when the paps realised that I wasn't the scorned wife they yelled at me anyway as I waited for the security gates to open. 'How's Alysha? Is she heartbroken? How are the children? Are they devastated?' Television vans blocked the street, and there was a line of tents on the nature strip where reporters had obviously been camping all night. They even had gas stoves brewing tea and a portable barbecue on the corner cooking sausages. Sensing this scandal could stretch on for a while, these guys weren't going anywhere soon.

Once safely inside the property, I wasn't surprised to see the cars of Alysha's agent, publicist and lawyer parked in the driveway. The reality television trucks were also still present. The producers would be ecstatic about this unexpected plot twist. There was nothing like a juicy affair, not to mention a possible love child, to hook viewers.

'Lindsay, you're back!' cried Alysha when I walked into the kitchen. 'I've been trying to get hold of you *all* day.' The children were sitting on the floor colouring in photographs of their father, which someone had printed off the internet for them. The entire scene was utterly surreal.

It was the first time I'd seen my boss without make-up, and she looked far softer and prettier than usual, even with dark circles under her eyes and blotchy cheeks from crying. The thought crossed my mind that a magazine would pay thousands of dollars for a photograph of her right now for their 'stars without make-up' section.

The general public *love* seeing celebrities looking terrible but the truth is, even when you live with a star, you rarely see the 'real' them. These women wear make-up morning, noon and even overnight. I don't think even Alysha's children had ever seen her without make-up before.

Although it's rare, I do have evidence of a few famous mums in their natural state. On my laptop I have a photograph of Steven Stavros's second wife, Jamie. In the picture she has no make-up on and her mouth is hanging open because she's yelling at a cleaner. A magazine would have a field day. They could run it next to one of Jamie's modelling shots, with a big 'before and after' headline. Yet, even though Jamie was the boss from hell, I still haven't sold her out. Nor have I deleted the photo, though—I like to keep it just in case she ever breaks Steven's heart.

Without her cosmetic mask I found Alysha far less intimidating and instantly more likeable. She looked even tinier than usual, wrapped in a Gap hooded sweater, which was the most unstructured item of clothing I'd ever seen her wearing.

I considered how hard the last few months must have been for my boss, knowing that soon the whole world would know her business and probably see her as a victim. No wonder Sir Cameron had been reluctant to let the reality television crew visit him in Morocco, and had guarded his privacy so fiercely. This was clearly the skeleton that he'd been hiding in this study.

'Is it true that he had an affair?' I couldn't believe I'd been brave enough to ask the question. This was seriously overstepping our usual boundaries, but Alysha's vulnerability made me feel bolder.

Alysha looked shocked for a moment, and then just defeated. 'Yes, it's true,' she said. 'He came clean almost a year ago. It was just before we hired you, actually. He said he planned to divorce me but wanted to wait until his next movie came out before making it public. That would have given me a few more months to prepare myself. But now she's . . . now she's . . . now she's . . .' Alysha sunk her head onto the countertop and dissolved into sobs.

From her position on the floor, Harlow helpfully filled me in on the details. 'Daddy is having another baby,' she piped up from the floor, 'but it's only going to be half a baby to us, because it's not being made in our mommy's tummy.'

So the rumours were true. Sometimes magazines do get it right. This meant that Alysha's ordeal was far from over, as the press would have at least eighteen months of juicy material before they lost interest—photos of each stage of the pregnancy, the baby shower, the birth and the child's first birthday. Journalists and the general public don't get bored with stories like this quickly.

As Alysha continued to sob onto the table, I stood frozen at the entrance to the kitchen, desperately wanting to hug her. The problem was, Alysha had written a 'no touching' clause into her contract. I was allowed to make physical contact with the children but I was never allowed to lay a finger on her, even to brush a piece of dust off her shoulder.

The only other adults in the room were her agent, publicist and lawyer, and none of them reached out to hug her either. I wondered where Alysha's real friends were, and whether her mother was on her way. It must be sad when your support network is your staff, who aren't even there by choice.

It reminded me of the time Rosie was hired by the wife of a businessman who worked away from home 230 days of the year. The couple's son was seventeen years old, so Rosie was surprised they'd even hired a nanny as he was fully self-sufficient. She was also surprised when the mum started inviting her on shopping trips and to dinner, or to see a movie. The teenage son was never interested in going with them, and Rosie would joke that it felt like she and the mother were dating. It soon became clear that the mum was desperately lonely and really just wanted a friend-for-hire. Her teenager didn't need a babysitter but she was willing to pay $400,000 a year for a companion.

Alysha had never tried to bond with me in this way, but I still found it hard to watch anyone suffer. I'd never met Sir Cameron so didn't feel any loyalty to him, but I'd shared a home with Alysha for over a year, and this made us family, in a sense . . . sort of.

Suddenly my boss raised her head and shrieked, 'I have got to get out of here! I feel like a prisoner.'

Her agent, who'd spent the last ten minutes checking Facebook on her mobile, finally spoke up. 'I really don't think that's a good idea, Alysha,' she argued. 'We should wait until you're feeling better to make your first public appearance.' We all knew that she really meant 'we should wait until you're looking better'. Alysha's publicity team would want to choreograph every moment of her big reveal. I bet Fernando had already been emailed a brief, asking him to submit ideas for a make-up look that matched 'heartbreak chic'.

'My husband has *knocked up* an *actress*!' yelled Alysha. 'I am not going to get over this overnight, and I can't stay in this house forever while he's on the other side of the world *gallivanting* around, playing happy families.'

At this point I excused myself to go to the bathroom, so I could splash cold water on my face and try to think straight. I'd been awake since 4 a.m. and my jetlag was starting to kick in.

I was also still reeling from my argument with Will, who hadn't contacted me to apologise before I left, despite the fact I'd seen him drive past my house three times, while I peered through my bedroom curtain. I also felt guilty for neglecting my parents during my trip back, although they insisted they understood. 'What a weekend,' I told my reflection in the mirror. Little did I know, it was about to get even more bizarre.

•

'Lindsay, you're going to be my decoy.' It had been a mistake leaving the kitchen because by the time I returned Alysha had come up with a plan, and it all revolved around me.

'We need a way to distract the paparazzi,' she exclaimed. 'You can pretend to be me and then I can sneak away.' I was to put on one of Alysha's outfits and drive her Mercedes out of the front gate so that the paparazzi herd followed me.

She thought it was a stroke of genius. I thought she'd had too much coffee.

Unfortunately, her agent, her publicist and her lawyer were in agreement. She'd even summoned one of the reality television cameramen, who'd agreed to sneak her out of the gates in the back of his truck—on the proviso they were allowed to film her great escape.

I could have said no but my conscience got the better of me. My purpose as a nanny is to look out for the wellbeing of the children, and that included making sure the woman who gave birth to them didn't have a breakdown in front of them.

So I followed Alysha to her bedroom, where she dressed me up as her doppelganger. Once I had on Alysha's leather jacket, oversized Gucci sunglasses and a Karl Lagerfeld leather baseball cap, I did look surprisingly like the soap star herself.

'I think I'm as ready as I'll ever be,' I said to Alysha, giving her a twirl, but she reached out to stop me before I left the bedroom. She slipped her wedding band and diamond engagement ring from her finger and handed them to me.

'It's all about the attention to detail,' she explained. 'The photographers will zoom in on your finger because they'll want to see if I'm still wearing my wedding ring. This will convince them that you're me.'

I had to hand it to Alysha. Even in her hour of need, she knew how to play the game. I didn't think I'd given her enough credit.

As I drove out of the driveway in a Mercedes with the personalised number plate that read '90210', the paparazzi leapt to attention. When they spotted a flash of blonde hair through the tinted windows, they jumped into their own vehicles. Soon I was being followed by a fleet of cars as photographers raced to get the first photograph of the starlet nursing a broken heart.

Luckily this wasn't the first paparazzi chase I'd ever been in. 'You've trained for this moment, Lindsay,' I muttered to myself. 'You can do this.' It was time for my training in defensive driving to come into action. Whether you're dodging photographers or an assassin, the basic skills are the same. You can't freak out when a car is tailgating you. It's important just to keep calm and think three steps ahead.

'Just keep driving until I call you to say I'm clear of the house,' Alysha had told me. I was glad that she had a full tank of petrol. I wished the traffic wasn't so heavy, because every time the car stopped or slowed down a different member of the pack would pull up beside me and try to take a photograph.

I pulled down the visor of my cap and hoped that the car's tinted windows would make it impossible to get a clear shot. I wondered how many magazine covers 'fake

Alysha' would be on the next day. That would be one for my scrapbook.

This wild-goose chase went on for nearly an hour. Gradually the paparazzi got bored and dropped off until only two cars remained. They were driven by two eager paparazzi in their early twenties, who'd probably been warned by an editor that their jobs depended on getting a photograph. I could see them both talking on their mobile phones, probably to each other. Sometimes the paps work together to get an exclusive shot and then split the profit.

I couldn't quite believe what happened next. As we drove onto a stretch of highway where the traffic split into three lanes, the two cars sped up to overtake me, one on either side, like I was in a sandwich. Then, to my astonishment, they both turned into the centre lane and collided head on with each other, right in front of my car. The crushing of their bonnets was deafening, and I slammed on my breaks just in time to avoid hitting them.

There was no doubt in my mind they'd crashed on purpose just to force me out of the vehicle. I'd heard about underhand tactics like this before, but it was the first time I'd been on the receiving end.

As smoke billowed from their crushed bonnets, the paparazzi quite calmly got out of their cars, with their cameras still in hand. They'd managed to position the cars so they blocked the entire road, a one-way street, so there was nothing I could do but wait. With shaking hands, I locked the doors of my car. There was no way I was getting out until the police arrived.

I decided to take my own advice. 'Just play the game. It isn't real,' I muttered. I turned up the radio, closed my eyes and tried to imagine that I was back home in Hamilton. I was lying in a field near my parents' house, feeling the grass on my back and the sun on my face.

My fantasy was so effective that I fell asleep for a moment, until I was woken by a *tap tap tap* at my car window. I expected to look into the face of a policeman or one of the photographers, but to my astonishment I found myself looking into the eyes of Tommy Grant. To be honest, he looked just as astonished to see me as I was to see him.

'Lindsay, is that you?' he asked as I wound down the window a centimetre. 'I was a few cars behind you and recognised the number plate, but I thought it was Alysha driving. The kids aren't with you, are they?' He peered into the backseat of the car and looked relieved when he saw that it was empty.

'No, I'm on my own,' I said. 'But the paps think I'm Alysha. It's a long story, but I've got to get out of here before any more reporters arrive. They'll have a field day with all of this.'

Tommy looked thoughtful for a moment. 'Leave it with me,' he said, and marched over to the pair of lurking paparazzi, who turned their camera lenses on him. This story was getting better and better in their eyes—a famous golfer rescuing a heartbroken soap star from a car crash.

I watched as Tommy gathered the photographers in a huddle. As he spoke I saw their faces change from sceptical to interested and finally to delighted. They then put the lens caps back on their cameras and retreated to their vehicles.

Frantically, Tommy signalled for me to get out of the car and follow him. I did as I was told, wondering what he'd planned with the slimeball photographers. Whatever it was, my instinct told me to trust him. 'Ready to leg it?' asked Tommy, glancing down at my sneakers.

He grabbed my hand and we ran, weaving through the traffic jam that had been caused by the paparazzi pile-up. We didn't stop running until we reached a taxi rank, where he opened the door of a cab and bundled me inside. He then handed a wad of banknotes to the driver. By the time I got my breath back, the taxi was speeding back to Alysha's house and my rescuer was far behind us. I couldn't even remember saying goodbye to him.

My head was still spinning the following morning when I logged on to The Daily Juice website, expecting to read about Alysha's near-crash. It seemed that my boss could breathe easily for a moment, however, as a new piece of gossip had captured their attention.

'GOLFING GOLDEN BOY SPLITS FROM GIRLFRIEND,' screamed the headline. 'Sports star says he's a dating disaster.' Under a photograph of Tommy looking wistfully at the camera were the names of the two paparazzi that had got the exclusive. It seemed that Tommy Grant had thrown himself into the fray for me.

I wanted to thank him, but I had no way to get in touch with him. Contact details were closely guarded secrets here in Hollywood. More than that, I desperately wanted to know why Tommy had made such a sacrifice for me, in this town where reputation was everything. He'd laid his own privacy on the line for me . . . and I had no idea why.

15

To Lindsay Starwood and guest

Will Marsden & Heidi McPherson
request the honour of your presence as they join their
hands and lives in holy matrimony.

Please help us to celebrate this very happy union.
Saturday 26 August
Town Hall, Hamilton

It was starting to feel like my world revolved around marriages and break-ups. The term 'whirlwind' didn't even start to cover it. It had been six weeks since Sir Cameron had officially left Alysha and since then life had moved at breakneck speed. The divorce had already been finalised and Alysha had got the house, custody of the kids, a hefty monthly allowance and a 10 per cent cut of the profits from all his future movies. She also kept her wedding ring and the Fabergé egg they received as a wedding gift. Hell hath no fury like a woman with a vicious divorce lawyer.

I was actually responsible for hooking Alysha up with her divorce lawyer, Ivan Sandy, who was the go-to guy for scorned wives in Hollywood. (Alysha had decided her usual lawyer didn't have enough 'break-up' experience.) As you can imagine, he was never short of business. He could find a loophole in any pre-nup and was not afraid to use dirty tactics. According to Fernando, who had been desperate to know the details, Alysha had threatened to leak a story about her husband's 'unusual' sexual preferences to the press if he wasn't accommodating. The whole deal was signed and sealed within a week.

A quickie divorce was in everyone's interest as Cindy Berry hit her third trimester. Sir Cameron and his new leading lady made their first public appearance as a couple at the Met Gala. They didn't have to confirm the pregnancy, because her bump spoke for itself.

I'd heard through the grapevine that they'd already hired a nanny, who'd been told to update her passport so she could spend two weeks in France with them the following summer. I suspected this meant they were planning to get married. A lot of celebrities fly to France to get hitched, because the paparazzi laws are stricter there, and photographers can't get away with flying over the venue in helicopters or hiding in the crypt of the church.

Alysha was dreading the moment the pregnancy was confirmed, but it actually worked in her favour, thanks to a slip-up by Cindy. The mum-to-be had agreed to give an interview to The Daily Juice on the proviso that she only talked about her latest movie, not her private life. Unfortunately, her agent had underestimated Caesar's powers of persuasion.

'CINDY BERRY CALLS ALYSHA APPLEBY A "FAILURE" FOR NOT GIVING BIRTH TO A SON' screamed the headline the next day. Cindy claimed she had been misquoted, but the damage was done as women around the world turned on her. Meanwhile a 'Team Alysha' page was set up on Facebook, and she instantly earnt the sympathy of any woman who'd experienced infertility or infidelity.

Suddenly every television station and magazine wanted a piece of Alysha. She was a household name at last, but was acting unusually coy. 'I really, really don't want to talk about it,' I heard her tell her agent over the phone. 'I just *don't want to. Stop* asking me.' She finally accepted an invitation from Oprah, but said no to every other interview request.

I'd seen a distinct difference in Alysha since the divorce. She was far quieter at home and, instead of going out for dinner every evening, she had asked if she could eat with the children and me in the kitchen. 'Umm, Alysha, you don't need to ask my permission,' I answered. 'It's your house and they're your daughters.'

I even saw her eat a carbohydrate, when Koko fed her a piece of alphabet spaghetti from her fork. This was a miraculous event.

One evening I caught her watching Cherry and me as we played on the living room floor. I was tickling Cherry, who wiggled on the carpet, letting out happy snorts and giggles.

'Lindsay, can I ask you a question?' Alysha asked quietly. 'How do you know how to play?' It always amazes me how many parents don't have this natural instinct. If a director told Alysha to jump, skip or laugh she could do it for the cameras, but she had no idea how to create spontaneous fun. I had faith that she could do it; she just needed to be pointed in the right direction.

'Cherry,' I said. 'Why don't you sing your mummy the song I taught you yesterday? I'm sure she'd love to hear it.'

The song was 'If You're Happy and You Know It'. I know nannies who teach their kids pop songs, but I like to be more traditional, and that's always a crowd-pleaser. Both Cherry and her mother looked hesitant, unused to having each other's undivided attention.

'I've got an idea,' I encouraged. 'Why don't the three of us sing it together? Alysha, you must know the words from when you were a little girl. Come on, Cherry!'

I stood up in the centre of the room, took a deep breath and began to sing as loudly and tunelessly as I could manage. When I got to the first clap Cherry couldn't resist joining in, her pigtails shaking as she nodded her head in time.

I glanced across at Alysha and was amazed to see that she was blushing. This was a woman who'd allowed a reality television crew to film her pap smear, but was too shy to sing with her daughter. I silently wished she would let go and live a little. At first just her lips moved, as she mouthed along with the words, and then she grew louder and more confident.

Soon the three of us were belting out the song, stamping our feet and clapping our hands, as the reality television cameras continued to whirr overhead.

I once read a quote by an American journalist named Lester Bangs, who said 'The only true currency in this bankrupt world is what you share with someone else when you're uncool.' Maybe I should have this printed on a T-shirt for Alysha. From the look on her face, I'd be willing to bet that she'd have chosen that moment with her daughter over her entire divorce settlement.

•

I hadn't heard a peep from Tommy Grant since he rescued me from the paparazzi; however, that didn't mean I hadn't had any excitement in my personal life. I'd had a job offer, which in itself wasn't unusual, but it wasn't in my usual line of business.

I'd been invited to spend a fortnight on the superyacht of an Oscar-winning director called Roger Kane, but he didn't want me to spend time with his daughters; instead, he wanted me to spend time with his nannies. He'd requested that I act as their mentor and school them on how to handle privileged children.

I would be paid $850 per nanny, per day. That meant a pay cheque of over $71,000 for one fortnight's work. I'd also be flown to Hawaii, where the superyacht was docked.

'But I don't need to go,' I told Alysha. 'I'm just telling you about the job offer in case you heard it through the grapevine and thought I was hiding it from you. I wanted you to know that they approached me, I'm not job-hunting.'

I hadn't expected her to give me the time off when her home life was currently so unsettled. However, it helped that Roger Kane happened to be her ex-husband's biggest rival. If Roger's life was easier, that would make Sir Cameron's life harder. She also seemed genuinely excited to have the opportunity to spend extra time with her daughters. I had offered to find a nanny to cover my workload, but she insisted that she could take care of them.

'We don't need any more strangers in this house,' said Alysha. 'I'll see if their grandma can come and help out. It'll be nice to have a houseful of Appleby women for a fortnight.'

Eugenie was delighted and sent me a box of my favourite chocolates as a thankyou for leaving them. I tried not to be offended and hoped they'd want me back at the end of my working holiday.

The morning I left, the six sisters lined up in the hallway to wave me off in a taxi. Goldie had just given her mummy a makeover; Alysha's hair looked like a bird's nest, she had a pink heart drawn on her cheek in felt tip and a moustache drawn on in lipstick. After I kissed each child goodbye, Goldie piped up, 'Now it's your turn to kiss Mommy.'

Alysha and I exchanged glances, both looking as uncomfortable as each other as Goldie started chanting, 'Kiss, kiss, kiss,' with her voice getting louder and louder. I was about to step in and silence her when I saw Alysha—who'd been standing as still as a statue—flicker. Was she leaning in? Oh my god, she was! I was sure it would just be an air kiss, because of the no-touching clause, but our faces actually touched, and the children erupted into cheers.

It took all my effort not to laugh as Alysha blushed and looked away. She really wasn't used to public displays of genuine affection. As I closed the door of the taxi I heard Harlow say, 'Mommy, you're the only grown-up left!'

I predicted that while I was away for next two weeks instructing nannies in my yacht–classroom, Alysha would be learning plenty of lessons of her own.

•

'I'm a supernanny on a superyacht,' I thought to myself, as my helicopter touched down on the top deck of Roger Kane's floating mansion. To be counted as a superyacht a boat must be over seventy-nine-feet long, which is roughly the size of a tennis court. From my estimation, this boat was almost double that size. If I stood at one end I couldn't see the other.

A deckhand, who introduced himself as Josh, helped me off the chopper. 'There will be no one but staff on board until tomorrow,' he explained. 'You can set up your classes in the conference room or the movie theatre, or anywhere really. The entire yacht is at your disposal, so there's no shortage of options.'

During my career I've stayed on some of the world's biggest superyachts, owned by royalty, presidents and mining heirs. However, Roger Kane's $200 million mega-super-yacht was on another level. He co-owned it with his best friend, the CEO of a mobile phone company, and it was the ultimate boys' toy. It wouldn't be out of place in a Bond movie.

I tried to look unimpressed as Josh gave me a tour of the ship's seven decks, which included a rock-climbing wall, surf simulator and a rifle range. All the windows were bulletproof, the cinema was soundproof and the yacht was fitted with an 'anti-paparazzi laser shield' that was designed to detect and block camera lenses. The entire yacht was also fitted with sensors so the doors opened automatically when you approached them. There was an underwater garage where a mini-submarine was stored next to a limousine. According to Josh there was two million dollars' worth of art on board, which couldn't be insured because it was located at sea.

The name of the yacht was written on the outside of the boat in twenty-four-carat gold but had been chipped slightly during a recent trip to the Arctic. According to my tour guide, Roger preferred to sail in colder climates and felt more creative when in the presence of icebergs.

'Where is Roger now?' I asked Josh, worried that I wouldn't make the best impression if I bumped into my new boss in the denim jumpsuit I'd travelled in.

'Oh, he's in Egypt scouting a location for his next movie,' said Josh. 'He took the children so they could see the pyramids. They'll be no one but staff on board the yacht for the next few weeks.'

He laughed as he saw my stunned expression. 'Don't

look so concerned!' he said, 'This is a good thing. We've got no one to answer to.'

As this news sank in I felt a funny feeling in my ribs. I couldn't put my finger on it for a while, and then I realised that I didn't feel anxious. The unusual feeling in my chest was relaxation. For the first time in as long as I could remember I wasn't being watched by a parent or a security guard.

When I explained this to Josh his eyes lit up with mischief. 'So, how are you going to celebrate your temporary freedom?' he asked. 'I have some very good suggestions . . .'

It seemed the yacht's crew liked to party when their boss was away, and make the most of the ship's special features. 'The liquor cabinet is well stocked and the whirlpool is warm enough for skinny dipping,' added Josh. 'If we invite the security team to join in they'll turn off the cameras.'

However, I knew exactly what I wanted to do, and it didn't involve getting drunk or getting naked with strangers. There was only one way I wanted to rebel that evening. I planned to do the one thing that I could never ever do at home because I didn't want to upset the children, set a bad example or be caught on camera. It was the one thing I swore I'd never do in my boss's home, but now I was away and nothing was stopping me.

I said goodnight to Josh, went to my private cabin and shut the door firmly behind me. Then I sat on the floor and burst into tears. I let out the sob that I'd spent months and months suppressing. I cried like one of the children

I cared for, until I was hot, sweaty and exhausted. I cried in an ugly way, not pretty crying, like a damsel in a movie.

I wasn't even sure what I was crying for, but I certainly felt better afterwards.

16

LESSON 1
THE GOLDEN RULES FOR ELITE NANNIES

Know the mummy tribes

Wealthy mums fall into three different categories. The first is the 'absentee mother', who is always away from home, working, travelling or socialising. The second is the 'disconnected mother', who is physically at home but mentally not present. She can be in the same room as her children and still act like a stranger. I call the third category the 'nanny watchers'. These are the stay-at-home mothers who don't work and appear to do nothing, but still have a full-time nanny as well as housekeepers.

All three tribes share one factor—none of them want to admit to having a nanny.

Make sure you sleep

Re-energise yourself. When you're a live-in nanny you will work a lot more hours than you're contracted to. Even on your day off you're still on call, and you'll be woken at 6 a.m. by kids turning on *Sesame Street* or parents scream-ing down the phone. Grab sleep whenever you can, even if it's a half-hour break while you're waiting for one of the kids to finish their singing class. Being always on the go and being watched is exhausting, so bank sleep when you can.

Change the passwords on your phone and email regularly

In a high-security house you're on camera all day, every day, and a lot of them are positioned above your head, so they can easily see the passwords you're typing in to a laptop or iPhone. You don't want your passwords to fall into the wrong hands—whether it's your boss or a jour-nalist. (The security team aren't above taking bribes from reporters.) I change all my passwords every three weeks to be on the safe side.

•

I had my golden rules stuck to the wall behind me when the nannies arrived for their first class the next morning. I knew I had my work cut out when, during our first lesson, a nanny put her hand up and asked, 'Have you ever been to the Oscars?' I'd spent the last two hours talking about first aid procedures, so the question couldn't have been less relevant.

Sadly, I've met a lot of nannies over the years who have absolutely no caring instincts and really shouldn't be working in the industry. Some are lured in by the money, while others just love the idea of rubbing shoulders with celebrities. In a fair world, people wouldn't employ them, but many slip through the cracks, especially if they can speak a second language. Some parents would rather their child have a bilingual nanny than one who is proven to be loving and nurturing.

Of the six nannies I had to teach, four were in their early twenties and were relatively new to nannying. The remaining two were older than me and had actually been working in the industry for much longer. However, as I quickly discovered, the veterans were totally apathetic. And most of the newbies just wanted to marry a millionaire or become famous by proxy.

'We're going to start with the basics,' I told them. 'You might think this is obvious stuff, but attention to detail is important.' I gave every student a Baby Born doll to look after and asked her to show me how to change a nappy, how to rock the baby to sleep and how to make a bottle. Even these simple tasks were too difficult for some of the nannies. It wasn't that they were clueless so much as that they were easily distracted, constantly updating Twitter or checking messages on the dating app Tinder.

On our lunch break I found a Baby Born floating face-down in the swimming pool. The nannies were meant to carry the dolls around all day, caring for them as they would a real newborn. It was a test to see how well they could keep their attention on the job despite the salubrious setting, but it seemed their attention was waning. A 24-year-old nanny called Susie had accidentally knocked it in while repositioning her sun lounger so she could get a better tan.

Unfortunately Susie was sharing a cabin with a 33-year-old nanny called Lola, who seemed to be a bad influence. Lola had spent the past five years working for an eighties supermodel who was currently trying to make a comeback. 'I used to test shades of fake tan on the five-year-old's stomach,' I overheard her telling Susie. 'She had the same skin tone as me, so it was dead handy.'

The next night, over dinner, she revealed that she once spiked her boss's cookies with laxatives the week before a big photo shoot. 'What?' she said, when I glared at her. 'She shouldn't be eating cookies anyway when she's a model. I was just making sure she could fit into the dresses, otherwise she'd be on the warpath and I'd be in the firing line.'

By the end of the first week, I was growing more and more despondent. I really wanted to help these women but they didn't seem to want to learn. They were far more interested in Lola's juicy stories and trying to find out how rich I was. 'Do you have tons and tons of money saved?' Susie asked. 'My number one goal is to be a millionaire by my thirtieth birthday.'

I was so determined to bring them back down to earth that I found myself only talking about the downsides of nannying. Every time Lola boasted about a VIP party she'd attended, or the diamonds she'd been gifted, I'd tell them about the time I worked for three days straight without any sleep during the Oscars, or the mother who made me fly in economy with her children while she bought a first class seat just for her fur coat.

'There are six important points you have to remember,' I lectured. 'You must be tough. You must be flexible. You must learn to hold your tongue. You must have no ego. You will be abused, mistreated and walked all over. Most importantly, you are *not* paid to show emotion or to have an opinion. You are just the nanny—never forget that.'

Thinking about these bad moments was bringing me down, but I wanted the students to realise the reality of this industry. As I went back to my cabin at the end of the seventh day, I felt like crying again. I didn't feel like I had been a good teacher, and I missed the Appleby children. I was hoping they might have called or texted but I hadn't heard anything from them. I mentally kicked myself. *Who are you kidding, Lindsay? They're not your children. You're just the hired help.* The only email I'd received had come from my mother, asking if I'd RSVP'd to Will's wedding yet.

I always carry an emergency box of Hershey's Chocolate Kisses in my suitcase, to be given to the kids as bribes if they have a tantrum at the airport. Right now I was on the verge of a tantrum myself, so this counted as an emergency. I pulled my suitcase from under my bed and unzipped the 'secret' pocket under the base, between the wheels. But when I reached inside, instead of a hard box, I felt something soft. What on earth was this? Then I laughed out loud as I pulled out a teddy in the shape of a rabbit. It was a Doodle Bear—a teddy that you can write messages on in felt-tip pen. I always buy them for the children when they travel, so they can collect signatures and messages from people they meet when they're away.

This Doodle Bear had a tag around its wrist that said 'To the world's number one nanny' in Fernando's twirling handwriting. Tears welled up in my eyes as I saw that the bear's chest was covered in messages from the six Appleby sisters, with a little help from my best friend.

Goldie had written, 'You plait my hair the bestest.' Cherry had scrawled, 'I love you because you look like me. You have white hair and blue eyeballs.' A big pink heart had been drawn on the bear's chest with 'We miss you' written inside.

I couldn't have discovered the bear at a better time. It was just the wake-up call I needed. 'This is what I should be teaching them about,' I muttered, and reached into my suitcase for my laptop. I was awake until 3 a.m. making the slideshow, but I still felt energised the next morning and raring to go.

•

I asked the students to meet me in the movie theatre instead of on the top deck where we usually had our lessons. 'What about my suntan?' I heard Lola mutter under her breath, but I chose to ignore her. I had already uploaded my slideshow to the cinema's projector and couldn't wait to get started.

'I've spent the past week telling you how tough this profession can be,' I told my students. 'I wasn't exaggerating when I said that nannies need a thick skin, a lot of patience and nerves of steel. However, we're not robots. Compassion and kindness are also very important qualities.'

I pressed play on the projector, and a video of me with the six Appleby sisters filled the cinema screen. It was taken during our last trip to the beach, when they'd buried me up to my neck in the sand. I looked ridiculous, but happy, and the children were squealing with excitement. 'This is why we really do this job,' I continued. 'Today I want to share with you some of my most joyful moments.'

For the next ten minutes I showed videos and photographs of some of the children I'd cared for over my career. Every nanny has favourite children, even though we're not meant to admit it, and often it's the kids who are initially the most challenging who end up being the most memorable.

I showed a photograph of Timmy, a two-year-old who had never uttered a word when I started caring for him, even though his parents had taken him to the most expensive therapists in New York City. I'll never know why he decided he wanted to speak to me of all people, but I'll never forget the day he turned to me and said, 'Pick me up, please.' It took another six months of coaxing before he'd speak to any other adult, including his parents.

There was also Jordan, a seven-year-old British boy who was a total nightmare, to be honest. When I worked for his family I was covered in bruises from where he'd punch and kick me, and we just didn't seem able to connect. When his mum drove me to the airport at the end of my three-month contract I felt like a failure, even though his mother assured me that nobody had ever been able to get through to him. Then, as I walked through the departure gate, I heard a scream behind me. It was Jordan, running towards me with tears streaming down his face. 'I don't want you to go,' he cried, 'I'll miss you!' His mum was crying too, as it was the first time she'd seen him show any emotion aside from anger.

As I told these stories even Lola and Susie fell silent. At the end I showed a collage of letters, pictures and Valentine's Day cards that I'd been sent by children I'd cared for, who'd never forgotten me. Finally, I pulled out the Doodle Bear and passed it around. 'This is why being a nanny is a privilege,' I said. 'The pay packet is great, but making a difference to a child's life is even better.'

At lunchtime, as the students filed out to the dining room, one of the quietest girls in the class, a 23-year-old called Jemima, approached me. Unlike the other nannies she hadn't really joined in the gossip sessions. I'd noticed that, while the other girls read celebrity magazines by the pool, she spent her breaks reading a book on child psychology. I'd asked if she was okay on more than one occasion, as I worried she felt left out, but she always said she was happy, and would join the group when she finished the chapter she was reading, but never did.

'I wondered if I could ask you a favour,' Jemima said nervously. 'I'm friends with a few nannies working on other yachts in the harbour. I was telling them about your lessons and they'd love to come to class on Sunday, if you don't mind.'

When I agreed to Jemima's request, I'd expected an extra one or two nannies to turn up. But at 7 a.m. on Sunday I heard the buzz of speedboats outside my bedroom window. When I walked into the conference room, twenty nannies filled the first three rows of seats. I couldn't believe they'd given up their day off to listen to me speak. I looked at Jemima and she shrugged apologetically. 'Sorry, word spread fast.'

I was glad that I had a very special lesson planned for that morning. I was going to teach the nannies the secret of baby language, which allows you to understand why a baby is crying. It may sound unbelievable, but I am fluent in baby communication. There are eleven types of cry, which all have different meanings. 'Neh' means 'I'm hungry', 'Owh' means 'I'm sleepy' and 'Eairh' means 'I have gas'. It's tricky to master but a real timesaver once you're familiar with it.

Before that, however, the nannies had a request. 'Tell them the story of the little boy who couldn't speak,' said Lola. 'No, tell them about the British boy at the airport,' chimed in Susie. So I ran through my entire slideshow again, getting into my stride the second time around. At the end of the class I gave each of the new nannies my phone number and told them to contact me if they had any worries or questions.

If I could help even one nanny to be better at her job, and that nanny went on to care for twenty or thirty children in her career, then I would have made a real difference. It was the first night since my argument with Will that I didn't go to bed feeling completely despondent.

17

From: MelanieSchitz@official.com
To: lindsay.starwood@gmail.com
Subject: Elite Nanny Academy

Dear Ms Starwood,

I am writing to you on behalf of my client, a highly regarded businessman whose name I am not at liberty to reveal at present.

We understand that you recently ran a training course in Hawaii for a number of nannies. My client would be extremely interested in sending his current team of nannies to train under you. He feels they could benefit from your knowledge, guidance and expertise.

Could you please tell me when the next term of your nanny school begins, and send through the breakdown of your fees.

Yours sincerely,
Melanie Schitz
Executive Assistant

•

There's no nicer feeling than returning home and ringing the buzzer on the front gate to be met by kids throwing themselves at your legs. 'Lindsay is here! Mommy, it's Lindsay!' Even the reality television crew milling around the garden didn't annoy me as much as usual. I did notice that they seemed to be packing up their equipment, loading their props into the back of huge trucks and rolling up the wires that had webbed the garden for weeks.

As I hugged each child I noticed one big difference— they were all dirty. Lavender had a splash of mud across her forehead, and Goldie had leaves in her hair and grass stains on her white Ralph Lauren pants. They looked like 'normal' children who'd spent the morning playing, rather than a squeaky-clean commercial for laundry powder, which is how Alysha usually preferred them.

As I scooped them up in my arms Harlow shouted in my ear, 'Guess what, Lindsay! We're having a *party* and even Daddy is coming.' I tried to hide my surprise. 'Well, that's very exciting,' I replied. 'Let's go inside and you can tell me all about it.'

In the hallway of the house I was met by Alysha, looking happier than I'd ever seen her. 'Lindsay, so lovely to have you back,' she cried, sounding like she meant it. 'Did my babies tell you we're planning a celebration?' She pointed to the fridge, where an embossed invitation was attached by a magnet in the shape of a clapperboard.

'YOU ARE INVITED TO A DIVORCE PARTY' it read in gold letters. 'Sir Cameron Appleby and the former Mrs Alysha Appleby invite you to celebrate their separation. Help us to usher in the next chapter. It's never too late to live happily ever after.'

I must have looked shocked because Alysha burst out laughing. 'Why not?' she shrugged her shoulders. 'I can either become a bitter divorcee or face the fact that my marriage had been over for a long time. Cam and I still have a lot to be thankful for.' She gestured at the children, who were now engrossed in watching the chef ice a line of cupcakes for the party, designed to look like mini balls-and-chains.

I had arrived home just in time, as the party was being held that evening, and Sir Cameron, his new girlfriend and her growing bump were to arrive any second. As Alysha poured me a cup of coffee, which in itself was unheard of—I'd never seen her even boil a kettle before—she filled me in on the party details.

The dress code was 'outdated', which was kind of genius. Guests had been asked to dress in fashion that was no longer in vogue, or as a product that was obsolete. This was a breath of fresh air for celebville, where the focus was usually on shiny newness. To my amusement and amazement, Alysha was dressing up as a floppy disk. 'I know it makes my butt look huge,' she said as I placed the sandwich board over her head, 'but the kids helped me make it, after I explained to them what a floppy disk was!' The six girls were dressing as Care Bears.

The entertainment would be provided by the cast of *Divorce Party The Musical*, who were flying in from a theatre in Las Vegas. There would be a 'trash the dress' area, where women could bring their old wedding dresses, put them on a mannequin and pelt them with paint bombs. There would also be a pop-up therapist's booth where guests could spend five minutes with a 'psychologist' who was actually a comedian.

'I decided it was time I learnt to laugh at myself,' said Alysha. 'If people think it's inappropriate they don't have to come, do they?' I very much doubted she'd be short of guests, however. Most people love hearing about other people's break-ups, and this was a chance to see the couple—and the scarlet woman who broke up their relationship—playing dysfunctional happy families together.

My prediction was right, as by eight o'clock that evening the Applebys' driveway was full of limousines. 'This might be the only party in Hollywood history where guests actually arrive on time,' I said to Fernando. 'Everyone is desperate not to miss out on any of the gossip.'

It was also the first and last time that I met Sir Cameron Appleby, who arrived in a helicopter that landed on the tennis courts. Straight away I could see who wore the trousers in his new relationship, as Cindy Berry stepped out of the chopper with a face like thunder. 'I don't understand why we couldn't have detoured past the Jolies' on the way,' she complained loudly, ignoring the children who were shyly waiting to meet their daddy.

Naturally, the atmosphere between Sir Cameron and Alysha was a little awkward, but she put on a brave face, and at least the house was big enough for her and Cindy to keep a safe distance. Despite what was sure to be a memorable party, I was feeling exhausted, having left Hawaii just twelve hours earlier, so at 9 p.m. I snuck up to my bedroom for a few minutes' peace and quiet.

It didn't last, as Alysha came bursting into my bedroom behind me. 'You won't believe it,' she cried. 'The entertainment has just cancelled.' It seemed that the cast of *Divorce Party The Musical* had missed their flight from Vegas. 'Lindsay, everyone is gathering around the stage. They're expecting a spectacle. You have to *do* something, you have to *help* me!'

The house was overflowing with singers and actresses—surely one of them could offer their services. But I suspected that Alysha was too proud to ask her peers—however, it showed her personal growth that she wasn't too proud to ask me.

'You must have some hidden talent,' she said, sounding desperate. 'Sing, dance, tell jokes? I'm so, so sorry to ask you, Lindsay, but I don't know what else to do. Please think of *something*. I don't want to give Cindy Berry any reason to call this party and me a failure.'

I thought of how rejected I'd felt when I found out that Will had got engaged without telling me, and we hadn't even been dating. 'Okay, I'll think of something,' I heard myself saying. 'Just give me ten minutes and I'll work something out.'

As Alysha turned to leave my room, I pulled the glass of champagne from her hand and downed it in one. Usually drinking on the job is a no-no, but these were extenuating circumstances. My boss raised an eyebrow. 'I'll send you up a bottle,' she said.

•

I cannot dance for toffee and the only jokes I know are from Christmas crackers, so that really only left me with one option—I'd have to impersonate a singer. The problem was I couldn't pick anyone currently in the charts, as there was a good chance the actual singer would be at the party. Imagine how embarrassing it would be impersonating Britney in front of Britney!

I desperately scrolled through the names on my iPod, looking for an artist whose songs I knew the words to. I was about to give up when, on a playlist that I'd made for my mother, I found the answer. Did I really dare? Then again, did I really have another option?

As the party raged downstairs, I committed another nanny no-no by sneaking in to Alysha's bedroom and raiding her walk-in wardrobe. I assumed that she'd forgive me, seeing as I was only doing it to save her face. On one rail of her closet were all the costumes she'd worn when she appeared on *Dancing with the Stars*. I picked out the most over-the-top dress of the bunch. It was gold with huge shoulderpads covered in silver tassels.

I then headed to Alysha's bathroom, where I covered myself in fake tan that I prayed was the wash-off kind, back-combed my hair and assessed my disguise in the mirror. There were two things missing. I grabbed a pair of large, round cushions from my boss's four-post bed and stuffed them down my bra. With one more swig of champagne courage, I was ready to take the spotlight.

I had to text Fernando to fill him in on the crisis. 'How on earth do you get yourself into these situations!!!' he replied, which was exactly what I had been thinking.

As I tottered down the stairs in a pair of silver platform heels that Alysha had bought in a charity auction from a Spice Girl, I was glad the dress code was 'outdated', so at least I fitted in.

On the way to the stage I stopped to tell the band the song I'd be singing. 'Really? Are you sure?' the band leader asked, and then shrugged. 'Well, if that's what Mrs Appleby wants, that's what Mrs Appleby gets.'

My legs were shaking as I climbed the steps to the stage, which had been erected in the ballroom of the mansion. When I reached centre stage and looked down, I found myself staring into the faces of the toughest crowd in the world—from Oscar winners to multiplatinum performers and every judge from every TV talent show. Oh well, it was too late to back out now.

I put on my best country and western accent and spoke to the crowd. 'Well, howdy, people, I just flew in from Dollywood and I'm delighted to be here.' Thank goodness my mum idolised Dolly Parton when I was growing up, so I knew her entire backstory. I got into my stride as I told the crowd all about my life—how I grew up in the mountains and was one of twelve children. How I was so poor I used cracked raspberries as lip gloss and burnt matches as eyeliner.

I could see Fernando in the corner of the room doubled over with laughter, standing next to Caesar, who was filming the entire skit on his iPhone. Well, if I was going to be the lead story on The Daily Juice tomorrow I may as well put on a good show.

I reverted to my normal voice and said to the crowd, 'I'll tell you a secret—I'm actually the nanny.' I then pointed at Sir Cameron, who was standing in the corner of the room with his mouth hanging open. 'If only my boss would realise that I should only work nine to five.' Then with perfect timing, the band struck up the first chords of Dolly's iconic hit.

I strutted and hollered and, when the final chorus kicked in, I realised that the crowd were singing and dancing with me. Some of the women had kicked off their shoes, others were dancing around their handbags, and the children were leaping around ecstatically. Maybe it was the uncool dress code that helped them lose their inhibitions. Or maybe it was the sight of someone else making a complete fool of themselves. Whatever the reason, the most elite celebrities in Hollywood decided to dance, for one evening, as if no one was watching.

At the end of the song, when the guests broke into thunderous applause, I realised two things. First, that this had been one of the best nights of my life. Second, deep down I knew that it was also a finale, marking the end of my time with the Applebys, and also my career as a VIP nanny.

18

Heaven Scents Floral

Dear Dolly,

You are spectacular.

T.G.

I only discovered that Tommy was at the party two days later, when Alysha and I were looking through the official photographs. He had come dressed as a Rubik's Cube, which is why I hadn't recognised him on the evening. Then a huge bouquet of lilies arrived, with a note from the mysterious T.G. He'd also sent a bunch of six helium balloons with the children's names printed on them.

When the delivery boy said they were for me, I glanced

at Alysha and grimaced. The previous Valentine's Day, when a bunch of roses came addressed to me, she'd accused me of breaching my contract. I had to call up the florist to prove that Fernando had sent them.

But on this occasion Alysha laughed. 'Don't look so scared, Lindsay,' she said. 'I'm pleased that a guy realises how special you are. Besides, you can do what you like now. You don't work for me anymore, remember?'

The morning after the party I'd handed in my notice and shyly revealed my big plans to Alysha. 'I'm going to open an elite nanny academy.' Since my course in Hawaii word had spread fast, and I'd received a dozen emails from parents asking me to train their nannies. I did some research and discovered that, even though nanny schools exist, there aren't any aimed at the VIP section of the industry. There was a gap in the market, and I aimed to fill it.

It was the perfect solution, as I'd still get the perks of the job, but without any of the day-to-day drudgery. I would be working for myself, so I could plan my own schedule, and even take the odd weekend off. I had also calculated that, if business was consistent, I wouldn't have to take a pay cut. If I did need a financial top-up I could always take a short-term nannying job to boost my income. I'd just been asked to spend Christmas in Hawaii with the president of a European country, whose regular nannies got the festive season off.

I'd drawn up a business plan with the help of Crystal, who was a whiz when it came to finance as well as social media. I would run an intensive two-week training course, but would also recommend that nannies sign up to an ongoing mentoring scheme where they could email or call me with questions. This meant I'd have an ongoing means of income, and I knew better than anyone that a nanny never has a shortage of worries.

I dreamt of creating a team of invincible supernannies who I'd dispatch to rich children in need around the world. In my head they looked like Charlie's Angels carrying nappy bags; action heroes ready to protect and serve. If I had anything to do with it, in a decade's time, you'd never again read an article about a rich kid who has gone off the rails.

•

'We're going to be friends forever,' I promised the children as I prepared to leave the Appleby household for the last time.

It sounds like a cliché, but this is the hardest part of the job for any nanny. Just ask any parent if they can imagine saying goodbye to their children forever, and they would find the idea out of the question. I'd helped to raise these children and now I had to walk away.

'Take care of my little ones,' I said to Opal, who I was delighted to have recommended as my replacement. She would find working for Alysha easy after her last employer, who had recently quit rehab and was making her staff's life a misery. Apparently she'd moved in with her new boyfriend, Rex, a punk rocker she'd met in the twelve step program.

'Lindsay, please keep in touch,' said Alysha. 'I really mean it. The girls will miss you. And . . . well . . . I will as well.'

'I'll miss them too, Alysha.' I smiled at my boss with genuine affection. 'I'll miss all of you.' The last month had seen a real shift in our relationship. Oh, Alysha and I would never be besties, but now, if I was asked to sum up my former boss in a word I wouldn't say 'diva'. I'd be more likely to say 'misguided'. Her heart really was in the right place, and even thought she struggled to connect with her children sometimes, I could see now that she really did love them.

Since I'd handed in my notice, I'd been waiting for Alysha's lawyer to arrive with a steel-tight confidentiality agreement for me to sign, but she hadn't. 'Oh, what's left to hide,' said Alysha, when I asked her. 'Once this reality show comes out, I won't have a private life left.' The premiere of her reality show was in one week's time at the glamorous ArcLight cinema on West Sunset Boulevard. I'd overheard Alysha asking her mother if she'd go as her 'date' for moral support. Eugenie seemed to have become her new confidante and, to the children's delight, was at the house every other day. I wondered if Alysha had any regrets about signing up to the fly-on-the-wall documentary, but I wasn't brave enough to ask. Even if she did, I suspected she had an ironclad contract with the television network.

It took seven removal men and three removal vans to transfer my wardrobe from Alysha's house to Fernando's sprawling apartment in Beverly Hills, where I'd be staying. (What can I say? I've amassed a lot of outfits during my time here.) Luckily there was a lot of closet space at my new home, as I'd have it to myself. Fernando and Caesar had just got engaged. Caesar proposed in a typically dramatic fashion, by hiring a flash mob to accost Fernando on his way to work, with a choreographed dance routine to Barbra Streisand's 'What Are You Doing the Rest of Your Life?'. Naturally he made sure a photographer was on hand to capture Fernando's shocked tears (and euphoric 'yes').

The happy couple were heading to England for three months while The Daily Juice launched a British version. 'Do you know our proposal video is the most-clicked post The Daily Juice has had this year?' boasted Fernando, flashing the huge diamond ring on his finger. 'I wonder if we could get married at the Tower of London ... imagine the photos!'

'Don't you dare stay there permanently,' I warned, as I helped him fill six enormous packing cases with his beauty essentials. 'As your maid of honour, I demand you have a Hollywood wedding, so I can help you taste-test wedding cake and argue with the flower arrangers.'

'You should think about moving to Britain next, Linds,' retorted Fernando. 'There's no shortage of cashed-up tots over there. And you never know, me and Caesar might need your services ourselves one day ...'

Ah, so the rumours were true. The previous week the *New York Post* had run a story about Caesar's plans to adopt a baby. I hadn't told Fernando, but I was already planning a trip to England anyway. I was secretly hatching plans to open a British branch of the nanny academy. Alysha had already recommended me to some of her famous friends in London, including the members of a girl band who had recently all had babies in short succession. I'd even received an email with a royal emblem, asking me to attend an interview for a childcare position with a certain future king, despite the prince and princess saying they were 'anti-nanny'.

It helped that my profile had been given an unlikely boost by the video of my Dolly Parton performance, which had gone viral, with over 700,000 hits on YouTube. My performance had been shown on every morning television show, and *Saturday Night Live* had even written a skit about it, with the real Dolly Parton playing me.

I was so distracted planning my new, exciting adventure that I had pushed all thoughts of romance to the back of my mind. I still hadn't spoken to Will, and I hadn't heard from Tommy since the day after the party. But this wasn't the time to be distracted with boy problems.

'Have you come up with a name for the business yet?' asked Fernando as he taped up the last packing box. It was on the top of my to-do list but I just hadn't been able to come up with anything snappy, despite a number of brainstorming sessions with Fernando. 'Nanny School' sounded too serious, 'The Nanny Guru' sounded too egotistical. I wanted a name that hinted I was skilful but also didn't take myself too seriously.

'I know, I know, I have to come up with it soon,' I grimaced. 'My web designer keeps emailing me every day because he wants to starts designing my logo. I just have this feeling inspiration will strike soon and I don't want to rush into it.'

•

Two weeks after I left the Applebys I was sitting at my desk when the doorbell rang. 'Hang on, I'm coming!' I hollered. When I quit nannying I thought that I might miss having household staff, but in fact I loved being alone, not having chefs and chauffeurs to juggle. It was all so simple.

I didn't think it was possible, but I was busier now than when I was a live-in nanny. I spent eight hours a day barricaded in Fernando's study, excitedly writing lesson plans and answering questions from parents across the world who were interested in sending their nannies to me. I felt like I was a different person. I had even bought a pair of horn-rimmed glasses, because they made me feel 'teacher-y'.

As I skipped down the hallway I saw the outline of a man's silhouette in the doorway and assumed it was a delivery man. I knew my mum had sent me a care package with kikki.K stationery for my new office. She was so proud her daughter was an 'entrepreneur'. I threw open the front door, expecting to see a uniform and clipboard.

'*What the hell?*' I felt like I'd been doused with a bucket of cold water. 'What on earth are you doing here?'

Will looked thinner and paler than the last time we met, although that might have been the jetlag. His jeans and checked shirt were crumpled and I suspected he'd come straight from the airport, as he had a large backpack at his feet. I did some fast mental calculations. 'Aren't you meant to be getting married next weekend? And how do you even know where I live?'

'Your mum gave me your address,' he answered. 'Lindsay, I saw that video of you singing on the internet and since then I haven't been able to stop thinking about you. I think I've made a terrible mistake. Lindsay, I'm in love with you.'

I'd clearly been living in Hollywood for too long, because my first thought was 'This would make a great romantic comedy.' My childhood sweetheart had travelled across the world to declare his love for me. It was the ultimate romantic gesture . . . so why didn't I feel euphoric?

At one stage I'd been so sure this was what I wanted, but something didn't feel quite right.

'How can you say you're in love with me when you think my life is ridiculous?' I asked. 'How can you want to be with me when you think I'm a gold-digger? Isn't that how you described it?'

A look of confusion crossed Will's face. It seemed he'd been expecting me to fall into his embrace. 'But this isn't the real you, Lindsay,' he replied, gesturing to the apartment and my Ferrari California in the driveway. 'You're not part of this world. None of it is real—can't you see that? It's just a bunch of silly people living in a bubble.'

I thought of Fernando, my nanny friends and all the children I'd cared for, who were surrounded by fame but were loving and loyal. Even Alysha just wanted acceptance. Who were we to judge her? I'd spent a decade with 'silly people' like this, and they'd taught me more about myself than I ever thought possible. I'd learnt how strong and patient I could be under pressure. I'd learnt that money can't buy you happiness, but it can make life a whole lot more comfortable. Most of all, I'd learnt that I wanted to be a mother myself one day—but not with Will.

'Thank you for coming, Will,' I told my oldest friend. 'But I think it's time you went back to your fiancée. I really don't need to be rescued. If I ever want to leave this town, I can find my own way to the airport and carry my own luggage.'

I glimpsed Will's expression turning to shock as I closed the door in his face. His hero moment clearly hadn't gone the way he had planned. I felt like I was walking in slow motion as I made my way back to my office, hearing Will calling my name behind me. It was all so surreal. I half expected to see a television camera whirring in the corner, and a producer who'd scripted a speech for Will to follow.

And then suddenly the fog in my mind cleared and I knew exactly why Will's declaration of love hadn't felt like the music was swelling and credits were rolling, like I'd always thought it would. *Where is it, where is it?* I shuffled through a pile of papers on my desk and unearthed the card that had been attached to the bouquet of lilies. I grabbed my mobile and dialled the phone number written at the bottom of it.

I wasn't surprised when it went straight to voicemail, because nobody in Hollywood answers calls from numbers they don't recognise, so I left a message.

'Tommy, I'll take you up on that date. But I want fish and chips on the beach, and I'll pay for my half. Let's make it Sunday.' If I was going to date a megastar then I'd do it on my terms. Tommy Grant could keep his wealth to himself, as long as he had a heart of gold.

Suddenly, I also knew exactly what I wanted to call my business. I grabbed a piece of paper from the printer and reached into my desk drawer for a pen, but pulled out a pink colouring crayon. Oh well, that seemed appropriate. At the top of the paper I scrawled in an arch 'The All-Star Nanny Academy'.

I wanted to groom the next generation of nannies to understand they're just as important as the VIPs who hire them. A nanny may never receive an Oscar or a standing ovation, but we're a vital brick in Hollywood's streets of gold.

I didn't know exactly where my career would take me next, but I planned to rip up the script and do things my way. It was time to be the leading lady in my own life. Lights, camera, action!

Acknowledgements

This book is dedicated to nannies around the world—whether you're caring for children in Hollywood, London, Paris or New Delhi. I wanted to write this book to show that we don't just spend our days playing pat-a-cake and hide-and-seek. Our role is important, complex and often dangerous. Our work is often underestimated and undervalued.

It's easy to think that the amount we earn and the perks of the job make us privileged and pampered, but it's good, solid work that we do each day. This job requires you to be unselfish, kind, compassionate, flexible, brave, reliable and strong. There are weeks when we feel helpless, lonely and just want to pack it in. But we don't, and that's what makes us the best at what we do.

There are many important jobs that exist behind the scenes that most people will never hear about—laboratory technicians who spend years developing life-saving machinery, pilots who hold the responsibility of flying people safely around the world, and personal assistants who carry out the hard daily grind so that their bosses can always appear cool and in control. Of course, nannies fit into this group too. Nannies thrive on the satisfaction of seeing happy and healthy little faces smiling up at us. We have a wonderful opportunity to help a growing population of the most beautiful humans on the planet. I'm privileged to have worked with many wonderful children throughout the course of my career.

I put up with difficult bosses and extreme demands because of the payback, both emotionally and financially. A career as an elite nanny can leave you rich in heart and mind, as well as in pocket.

I hope my nannying friends don't think that I have sold out by writing this book. In revealing the weird world that we inhabit, I wanted to paint them as heroes. I'm sure elite nannies everywhere will have very similar experiences to my own, and I hope that they will be able to laugh at my experiences and be relieved they're not alone.

I haven't broken the nanny code of ethics, because I haven't named and shamed any of my employers or their children.

I want to thank my former bosses, who knew that I was working on this book and were supportive. Some of my previous employers will recognise elements of themselves in the book, but all of the characters are works of fiction.

Philippa Christian

Philippa Christian has worked as a nanny for the rich and famous. Born and raised in Melbourne, she has lived and worked in Australia and worldwide. This is her first novel.